"Do you promise?"

She stood there, clutching her coat together over the bulge of her belly, as her eyes met Liam's, urging him to answer.

He hesitated, before returning his attention to her. "Promise what?"

"That you're offering me a legitimate job where I can earn my keep and that I won't be seen—or treated—like a charity case."

He nodded. "I promise."

Then he set his coffee mug on the porch rail, moved closer and slowly closed his hand around hers.

Mallory stood motionless, trying to adjust to the feel of his big hand enveloping hers. "Th-thank you for your kind offer, Liam. I accept."

"You're welcome, Mallory," he said softly.

She stood there, his hand covering hers, while a strong surge of fear and uncertainty urged her to break free and run. But this stranger—this man— standing in front of her thought she was brave, something she'd never truly felt before in her life.

She hoped, with every fiber of her being, that he was right.

April Arrington grew up in a small town and developed a love for books at an early age. Emotionally moving stories have always held a special place in her heart. April enjoys collecting pottery and soaking up the Georgia sun on her front porch.

Books by April Arrington

Love Inspired

A Haven for His Twins
An Orphan's Holiday Home
A Protector for Her Baby

Visit the Author Profile page at LoveInspired.com.

A PROTECTOR
FOR HER BABY

APRIL ARRINGTON

LOVE INSPIRED
INSPIRATIONAL ROMANCE

If you purchased this book without a cover you should be aware that this book is stolen property. It was reported as "unsold and destroyed" to the publisher, and neither the author nor the publisher has received any payment for this "stripped book."

LOVE INSPIRED®
INSPIRATIONAL ROMANCE

ISBN-13: 978-1-335-93705-6

A Protector for Her Baby

Recycling programs for this product may not exist in your area.

Copyright © 2025 by April Standard

All rights reserved. No part of this book may be used or reproduced in any manner whatsoever without written permission.

Without limiting the author's and publisher's exclusive rights, any unauthorized use of this publication to train generative artificial intelligence (AI) technologies is expressly prohibited.

This is a work of fiction. Names, characters, places and incidents are either the product of the author's imagination or are used fictitiously. Any resemblance to actual persons, living or dead, businesses, companies, events or locales is entirely coincidental.

For questions and comments about the quality of this book, please contact us at CustomerService@Harlequin.com.

® is a trademark of Harlequin Enterprises ULC.

Love Inspired
22 Adelaide St. West, 41st Floor
Toronto, Ontario M5H 4E3, Canada
www.LoveInspired.com

Printed in Lithuania

MIX
Paper | Supporting responsible forestry
FSC® C021394

Thou art my hiding place; thou shalt preserve me from trouble; thou shalt compass me about with songs of deliverance.
—*Psalm* 32:7

For grandmas, grannies, nanas, meemaws
and all the rest: thank you for loving us!

Chapter One

Mallory Kent no longer believed in New Year's resolutions. In past years, she'd made them with enthusiasm at the stroke of midnight beneath a burst of fireworks, hoping to improve her future. But soon the challenges of daily life—complete with all the obligations and pain—would resume, and every year she'd been left with the same feeling of failure. The same disappointment of losing more than she'd gained.

This New Year's Eve, she'd been left with two things in life. One, she didn't want. The second was the only thing of value left in her life.

Faith.

"Are you sure this is the place?"

Mallory glanced over her shoulder at the small sedan idling behind her in the darkness. One hour ago, the car had belonged to her. Now a stranger sat behind the steering wheel and the certificate of title, signed by Mallory, rested on the passenger seat she'd just vacated.

It wasn't the loss of the car that struck a deep chord of grief within her; it was the loss of the life she'd dreamed of having. A life full of love, family and safety with a husband who would protect rather than harm her. Leaving her home, belongings and job didn't coax the sting of tears to her eyes, but the loss of her well-being, trustful nature and personal dignity made her breath catch on a sob. And being forced to abandon everyone she'd known and loved to be able to live a peaceful life hurt most of all.

Blinking hard, Mallory fastened the top button of her long winter coat and tugged the plush hood lower on her forehead. Being adrift among strangers in unfamiliar surroundings with an uncertain future was…terrifying.

"Yes," she said. "This is it."

At least she thought so.

"Doesn't look like anyone's home." The woman behind the steering wheel lowered the driver's side window a bit more and leaned her head out, concern in her eyes.

Her complexion was bright and scarless—her face, most likely, had never felt the blow of a fist. Her gaze was clear, and her tone full of relaxed confidence.

All things Mallory used to possess…and never would again.

Jealousy and pain tore through her. Oh, how she wished she could go back. How she wished she'd had some kind of warning. How she wished others, like the stranger in front of her, knew how much they took for granted. How lucky they were to have lived a life of safety and security and to never have experienced the fear and pain she had.

Strangers like the woman before her meant well. They truly cared, said the right things and always offered to help, but they did so from the inside—a place of peace and protection—looking out at the suffering of others, never truly understanding. Because to understand was impossible unless they'd suffered through it themselves.

Mallory flinched and ducked her head. It wasn't right to feel this way. To resent the happiness and health of others simply because she'd lost her own. With each passing month, she could feel herself changing, becoming someone she no longer knew and, even worse, didn't want to know.

Immediately, she lifted her head, her lips parting to deliver an apology for her thoughts, to say something nice—anything to prove to herself that the kind, caring person she'd used to be still existed, somewhere deep inside.

"It's cold out," the woman continued. "You sure you don't want me to drive you into town? We passed a motel in Hope Springs not far from here. It looked like a nice enough place to lay your head for the night."

Mallory turned and studied the small cabin in front of her. There was a low glow in one of the front windows—the flicker of firelight, maybe?—and an ornate metal hummingbird, tacked beside the front door, was just visible in the gleam of the sedan's headlights.

"No, thank you," Mallory called out over her shoulder.

Log cabin, hummingbird sculpture. Forested seclusion among the Blue Ridge Mountains in North Georgia…

This was the place. Her new hiding spot. Or, hopefully, a starting point for establishing a new life somewhere safe. Safety was her top priority now. The unwanted responsibility she'd reluctantly taken on—after months of desperate prayer—had made it so.

Cheeks heating, Mallory lowered her head again.

"Well, if you're sure?"

Mallory summoned a polite smile, faced the stranger who sat in the sedan she no longer owned and nodded.

"Okay, then." The woman smiled. "Thank you for the great deal on the car. It's my New Year's present to myself."

Mallory patted the side pocket of her coat where she'd tucked a check for several thousand dollars safely inside. "Thanks for buying it so quickly. And for the ride. I know it must've been out of your way."

"No problem. I was happy to do it. Besides, now I can show off my new-to-me car to my friends at our party tonight." The woman smiled wider—a generous, carefree smile. "Happy New Year!" Her expression turned tender as her gaze lowered to Mallory's midsection. "I wish you both the best."

Mallory stiffened. Her weak smile vanished. She stood there, motionless, as the stranger backed the car out of the long dirt driveway. The headlights swept over the dormant lawn, the thick line of cypress trees, then settled on the paved highway before it disappeared into the night.

A brisk wind cut through the trees and shoved back her hood. She tugged it forward, exhaled heavily and watched the frigid wind break up the small white cloud of her warm breath.

"Just one step today," she whispered. "I'll take the next tomorrow."

Inhaling, she adjusted the strap of her small overnight bag on her shoulder, walked up the steps onto the porch and knocked on the front door of the cabin.

There was no response.

Goose bumps broke out over the back of her neck as cold wind cut through a gap between her ear and the hood of her coat. She glanced around at the dark, wooded surroundings. It wasn't late—only around seven thirty—but the early sunset and winter temperature made it feel like midnight. She tugged the strap of her overnight bag higher onto her shoulder, lifted her fist and knocked again, more forcefully this time.

A light flipped on inside the cabin, flooding through the front windows and pooling on the wooden slats of the porch beneath her tennis shoes.

Oh, what was her name? Mallory nibbled her chapped lower lip. Jennifer? Jessica?

Heavy footsteps approached on the other side of the closed door.

Jessie! That was it. Jessie Alden. The women's shelter was named Hummingbird Haven and its owner, Jessie Alden, lived in a cabin with a metal hummingbird hung by the door—this one. Jessie was the best at hiding women who didn't want to be found, or at least, that's what Mallory had been told.

The doorknob turned, wood creaked and the door swept open. She lifted her head and smiled. "Hi, I'm Mallory K—"

Her breath caught, choking her words. She stumbled back over the top step, one gloved hand fumbling for the porch rail, her hood sliding off her head.

"Whoa there." The deep throb of a man's voice barely penetrated the roar of her pulse in her ears. A big, masculine hand drew near, reaching for her elbow. "Caref—"

"Don't touch me!" She gripped the porch rail, steadied herself and forced her eyes to meet his.

They were hazel. A rich hazel dark with concern...or was it pity? How she'd grown to hate that look over the years.

"I'm sorry." He held his hands up, palms facing out, and stepped back. "I didn't mean to scare you."

She bristled. "You didn't."

His eyes held hers then his gaze roved over her face and lingered on her left temple. The concern in his eyes deepened.

Her face flamed. "I must have the wrong place." She moved down to the second step—slowly this time—and glared at his hands, her knees bent slightly, ready to bolt, if necessary.

"Wait."

The urgent tone in his voice forced her eyes back to his. She backed down another step.

"Sorry, I didn't mean to surprise you. Here, see for yourself. I've got nothing on me. It's just me." He lifted his arms out to the side as if to reassure her he wasn't a threat, exposing the wide expanse of his chest covered with a long-sleeved flannel shirt, and parted his long legs, encased in worn jeans, a couple of inches. His boots scraped across the wood planks of the porch with his movement. "I was only trying to help. To keep you from tripping over the steps. That's all."

The deep throb of his voice was soft, steady and calm. Concern still darkened his eyes and his expression was gentle. He returned her stare and remained motionless, save for the ruffle of his thick, blond hair in the wind.

He looked harmless enough.

A cynical laugh broke free of her chest and rose to her throat, but she clamped her lips together and swallowed hard, forcing it back. In her experience, appearing harmless wasn't a reliable measure of potential cruelty.

She had loved, trusted—and married—a man years ago who she thought was harmless, loving and kind only to discover he was the exact opposite.

"I assume you're looking for Jessie." He spoke softly. So softly, she could barely hear him over the whistle of strong wind between them. "She's my sister-in-law. She owns this place—Hummingbird Haven, I mean. I'm Liam Williams."

He lowered his arms then held out his hand. When she didn't reach for it, he returned it to his side.

"I'm in town, visiting Jessie and my brother for the holidays." He gestured to a dirt road that curved around the back side of the cabin. "She's out back at the community center with the residents, getting ready to ring in the New Year with fireworks. I told her I'd keep an eye on the cabin in case someone were to—" he gestured awkwardly toward her "—show up. I promise you, I'm only here to help."

"How can I know that?" The words burst from her lips before she could stop them. "I mean, for sure? How do I know?"

He tugged a wallet from his back pocket, opened it and held it out. "Here's my license so you'll at least know I am who I say."

She hesitated then ascended the top step and leaned forward, eyeing the license inside the open wallet under the porch light.

Liam Williams. 2971 Magnolia Lane. Pine Creek, GA.

She looked up, her eyes tracing the strong curve of his jaw beneath a blond five-o'clock shadow. "You...your brother's married to Jessie?"

"Yes. She and Holt were hitched two years ago." He flipped the wallet closed and returned it to his back pocket. "You said your name is Mallory...?"

"Kent." She licked her lips, which were now parched, the split flesh stinging beneath the moist touch of her tongue. "Jessie's having a party?"

"Of sorts. There are several women and children living in the cabins on the acres behind us. Jessie and my brother got everyone together, served a big dinner and planned on putting together a New Year's Eve fireworks display for them in an hour or so. Though with the wind blowing like it is, I doubt that'll come to fruition."

"Oh." Her throat tightened. "I don't mean to disturb the party but I need to speak with her, please. It took a lot for me to get here and I don't have a ride back, otherwise I'd never intru—"

"You're not intruding." He smiled gently. All kindness and compassion. "Please, come in." Seemingly harmless.

Mallory pressed her chapped lips together and focused on the sharp sting of pain. "No, thank you. Would you please get Jessie for me? I'll wait out here."

He hesitated, his eyes narrowing on her left temple then her chapped mouth. A strong gust of wind rocked her back on her heels and he frowned. "Wouldn't you rather wait inside?"

Shivering, she wrapped her arms around her chest and glanced over her shoulder at the darkness behind her. Then she leaned to the side and peered past him into the interior of the cabin. An overhead light lit up the living room, which had a large couch and a recliner. A fire burned bright in a stone fireplace.

"It's warm in here," he continued. "There's a comfortable couch near the fire and I just cooked up a fresh batch of soup for supper. You're welcome to enjoy both."

Her stomach growled at the tempting offer and she licked her cold, dry lips again. "Y-you're alone in there?"

"No." His smile dimmed. "My mother's asleep in one of the bedrooms."

Something in his tone had shifted. There was a heaviness to it. One of…regret?

Mallory studied his face. Sad shadows clouded his eyes. "She's not attending the party?"

"No," he said. "She's not comfortable around a crowd and if they do manage to have the fireworks show, she wouldn't enjoy them. The noise unsettles her." He shrugged and smiled again—forced this time. "As I said, it's warm inside and there's plenty to eat. Your wait for Jessie will be a lot more comfortable in the cabin rather than out here."

At her silence, he said softly, "I promise you're safe here."

Her eyes met his again, clinging, searching for the smallest sign that what he said might be true. That in this cold, violent world some modicum of safety and kindness remained and could be trusted. The thought of it—her belief in the tenuous possibility—was what had carried her here, after all.

A small, hopeful refrain whispered through her, echoing through her heart and mind. The sound of it had been her guide for months now and in this moment, she could either embrace it as she'd been doing, despite the presence of this unexpected man…or turn back and fall prey to the doubts that had plagued each step she'd taken forward.

Have faith.

Mallory glanced at the dark, empty night behind her once more, inhaled deeply and then, holding his gaze, forced her trembling legs to carry her inside.

Chapter Two

She was pregnant—very much so—and someone had hit her.

Liam clenched his jaw, followed Mallory inside the cabin and shut the front door. He kept his back to her, his hand tightening around the smooth doorknob as he drew in a calming breath.

He'd almost missed it—her thick coat had obscured the generous curve of her belly until she walked past him on shaky legs, clutching her overnight bag and tugging her coat tight across her chest. The material had stretched and clung to her protruding middle, drawing his attention.

The dark bruise on her left temple had been much more obvious—he'd noticed that right away—along with the slight swelling and discoloration around her left eye...as though the brunt of the injury had initially been inflicted there before fading with time. And the fear in her wide blue eyes and trembling frame had been almost palpable.

He was well aware of why Jessie established the women's shelter. He knew abuse occurred and how passionate his sister-in-law and brother were about helping women and children who'd fallen victim to it. He felt the same calling— to protect. That was why he hadn't hesitated when Jessie had asked him to stand watch at the shelter's intake cabin in the event that someone arrived, seeking help.

But knowing abuse occurred was different from coming face-to-face with the evidence of it…and he hadn't expected the surge of anger or disgust that rose within him at the sight.

Clearing his throat, he faced Mallory again and gestured toward the couch. "Please have a seat." He extended one hand slowly. "I'll take your bag, if you'd like?"

She studied his hand then her gaze traveled up his arm to his face, her eyes peering into his for a moment. "Yes, please."

Still moving slowly, he stepped closer and stretched his arm out. His fingers curled around the bag's strap as she passed it to him, taking care to avoid touching hers.

She nodded. "Thank you."

"You're welcome."

The fire crackled and she startled slightly, her hood sliding off her head as glowing embers sprayed against the iron fireplace screen.

"Nothing to worry about." He offered a small smile. "That screen's effective and the fireplace is up to code. Jessie used to live in this cabin with the twins before Holt renovated one of the larger cabins on a back lot for their new family and she never neglected anything."

She avoided his eyes. "She and your brother have twins?"

The thought of his rambunctious nephews widened his smile. "Yeah. They've got a toddler, too. A pretty little girl named Ava."

Her lips trembled and her hands seemed to move absently, lifting toward her belly then falling back to her sides without touching it.

Liam carried the bag across the room and sat it on the

floor, out of the way, then returned to the center of the living room. "May I take your coat, too? I imagine it's carrying some of the chill from outside and you'll warm up faster if you sit on the end of the couch, closer to the fire."

She stilled, stared at him then the fire, and nodded slowly. "Thank you."

Her fingers, stiff and clumsy, unbuttoned the buttons on her coat, then she slid it off and held it out. She wore a gray sweater, long and loose, that draped low, almost to her knees.

He took the coat from her just as he had the bag, taking care not to brush his fingers against hers, and she immediately walked away and sat on the end of the couch, nearest the fire and farthest from him.

"I'll give Jessie a call and get us some soup while we wait." He hung her coat on a coatrack near the front door. "Vegetable beef okay with you?"

She nodded and her big blue eyes widened as she glanced up at him beneath her thick lashes. Her legs, long and slender, bounced nervously against the front of the couch, and her hands, balled into fists, nestled below her belly, making the generous curve of her middle even more prominent.

She continued to steal glances at him, wariness in her eyes.

For an instant, a familiar mix of tenderness and hesitancy streamed through his veins, surprising him. It was a sensation similar to the one he had each time he welcomed a skittish mare to his farm for the first time—a warmhearted urge to soothe and reassure.

"Would you like a piece of cornbread, too?" He glanced at her belly then averted his eyes and remained motionless, allowing her to examine him openly with what he hoped would be a greater degree of comfort. "I always make it sweet—not spicy—on account of my mother's tastes." He smiled slightly. "She says the peppers give her heartburn—especially when she was pregnant with me. I'm not sure if it does that to you, but just in case…you know, on account of your pregnancy."

She didn't answer at first and the fire continued to fill the room with crackles and pops. He began to think she wouldn't answer at all but then—

"Yes," she whispered. "Thank you."

He looked up then and met her eyes. "You're welcome."

She turned away, facing the fire again.

Liam walked to the kitchen, tugged his phone from his pocket and dialed Jessie's number. She answered on the second ring.

"Liam!" Music and laughter sounded in the background. "You ready for Holt to take your place and stand watch for a while? If so, this is the perfect time." She laughed. "We've just started a round of limbo and the kids would get a kick out of seeing you try to shimmy your six-foot-three self under that low stick!"

Liam grinned. For years, he never thought his twin brother would ever settle down in one place, much less marry. A nomadic bull rider, Holt had left their family's farm when he'd turned eighteen and toured the circuit with no intention of returning home or mending the estrangement between himself and Liam. But after unexpectedly becoming a father, falling in love with Jessie and embracing God's new purpose for his life, Holt had become the strong, selfless, honorable brother, father and husband Liam always knew he could be if he put his mind—and heart—to it.

Liam thanked God every night for renewing his bond with his brother and caring, high-spirited Jessie, who had become the sister he'd always wanted. Holt and Jessie brought much-needed light and laughter into his lonely life, and they'd been pillars of support over the past two years as his mother's health had rapidly declined.

"I imagine you'd get a kick out of seeing me embarrass myself, too," he said. "And Holt would probably tell you to record it for posterity."

She laughed again. "Honestly? Yep. I would. And yes, Holt would probably ask that, too. So why don't you come on down and let Holt keep Gayle company for a while? It's time you had a break."

Liam's smile fell. He walked to the opposite side of the kitchen, farther away from the living room, and lowered his voice. "I can't. We have a guest. I need you up here, Jessie."

The music and laughter in the background faded, and the sound of a door opening and closing echoed down the line. A rush of wind sounded and the teasing tone in Jessie's voice vanished. "A woman or child?"

"Both."

"I'm on my way."

Liam disconnected the call, shoved the phone in his back pocket and grabbed two bowls from the kitchen cabinet. By the time he'd filled both bowls with soup, sliced generous portions of cornbread, gathered utensils and poured two glasses of sweet tea, Jessie had arrived.

She knocked once on the front door then entered, her gaze sweeping the room, meeting Liam's as he stood in the doorway of the kitchen, a glass filled with sweet tea in each hand.

"Thank you for coming so quickly, Jessie." Liam carried the glasses of sweet tea to the small table in the kitchen, set them down then glanced at Mallory, who still sat on the couch in front of the fire. "Mallory Kent, I'd like to introduce you to Jessie Alden, my sister-in-law."

Mallory, her face and neck now blushing a healthy pink from the warmth of the fire, stood slowly then walked across the living room and held out her hand. "Hi, Jessie. Thank you for coming to see me so soon. I'm sorry to have interrupted your party."

Jessie shook her head, her auburn ponytail slipping over one shoulder. "Please don't worry yourself. You haven't interrupted anything and I'm happy you came." She squeezed Mallory's hand gently then smiled. "But there is one thing I don't want to interrupt." She looked down at Mallory's round belly and smiled wider. "I imagine your little one's hungry for a warm meal right now and the smell of Liam's cooking even has me salivating."

Mallory looked down and stared at her belly. Her hands moved toward it briefly, without touching, then lowered to her sides as before. "It does smell delicious and it's been a while since I ate lunch." She glanced at Liam, her mouth curving slightly. "Liam's gone out of his way to make me feel welcome."

Liam grinned. The slight curve of her mouth—a vague resemblance of a smile—sent an unexpected wave of warmth through his chest. "Please have a seat." He gestured toward the table and the extra place setting he had arranged for her. "The soup's nice and warm. I have salt and pepper, milk or water if the tea's too sweet, whatever you might like." He glanced at Jessie. "Would you like to join us? I made plenty."

Jessie shook her head. "Thanks, but I'm stuffed to the gills. All the residents brought a dish to the New Year's Eve party. We'll have leftovers for at least a week." She walked over to the small kitchen table, pulled out a chair then beckoned for Mallory to sit. "I'd like to talk with you while you eat, Mallory, if you don't mind? I have some questions and am eager to help you in whatever way I can."

Nodding, Mallory walked over to the table and sat down. "I'd like that. Thank you."

Liam hesitated then asked, "Would you like some privacy?" He shrugged when Mallory glanced up at him. "I don't mind eating in the guest room if you'd be more comfortable speaking with Jessie alone?"

Mallory held his gaze, her eyes searching his, then returned her attention to the place setting in front of her. "No." She picked up the napkin beside her bowl of soup, unfolded it and laid it in her lap. Her hands, pale and graceful, still trembled. "Please stay. I'm the one who showed up unannounced and you've gone to a lot of trouble to make me feel comfortable."

He hesitated. "If you're sure?"

She glanced at him once more. "I don't mind if you stay. I'd hate to disrupt your meal."

He pulled out a chair, sat then propped his elbows on the table and folded one hand over the other. "I'll say grace." He bowed his head and closed his eyes. "Dear Lord, we thank you for your many blessings and the meal you've provided for us tonight. We ask that this food nourish and strengthen us so that we may continue to serve you."

A low rumble followed his last words.

Liam cracked one eye open and glanced at Mallory. Head bowed and eyes closed, she cringed as another growl emerged from her generous belly. Pale cheeks deepening to a fiery red, she quickly folded her hands in her lap, beneath the bulge of her belly, and her cute nose wrinkled.

She was adorable—surprisingly so.

Smiling, Liam continued, "We also thank you for bringing Mallory to our door tonight—for blessing Jessie and me with the opportunity to know her and enjoy this meal together and, hopefully, allow the three of us to enrich each other's futures. Your will be done. In Jesus's name, we pray…"

When Jessie and Mallory joined him on *Amen*, he opened his eyes, raised his head and inhaled the delectable scent of the soup steaming before him. "Smells delicious, if I do say so myself." He grinned at Mallory. "I'm as eager as you. Let's dig in, shall we?"

Her stomach rumbled again.

She lifted her head and smiled—a sincere one, this time—at his teasing expression. Despite the bruise that marred her left temple and the unfortunate circumstances she'd obviously endured, a flash of delight brightened her blue eyes and the hot flush in her cheeks receded, replaced by a pretty blush. "Yes. Let's do."

Brave *and* adorable. With the most beautiful smile he'd ever seen.

Liam ducked his head and redirected his attention to the food in front of him. She was extremely vulnerable. She—and her baby—were in trouble and she'd come here for help. His focus should be on ensuring she received that help. Allowing his thoughts to roam anywhere else—however innocent the territory—would not only be inappropriate and insensitive but disrespectful as well.

"So, Mallory," Jessie said. "Where do you come to us from?"

Mallory scooted her chair closer to the table then dipped her spoon into the soup. "Eton. It's a small town near the Cohutta Wilderness. A little more than an hour from here."

Jessie smiled. "I've heard of it. Never been there, but I'm told it's a beautiful community."

Mallory lifted her spoon to her mouth and closed her

eyes briefly on a soft sound of appreciation. "Mmm." Swallowing, she returned her spoon to the bowl and dabbed her mouth with the corner of her napkin. "It is. Very small—quaint—with mountains surrounding all sides." She ate another bite of soup then said, "Everyone knows everybody."

Jessie lifted one eyebrow. "Sometimes that's not a good thing. Is that so in your case?"

Mallory nodded. "My ex-husband lives there. We moved there to be close to his family five years ago. I was twenty-five at the time, had no family of my own and looked forward to settling down." She winced, picked up her glass of sweet tea and drank deeply, then added, "Starting a family."

Jessie glanced at Mallory's belly with a gentle expression. "It looks like you'll still be doing that."

Mallory's hand fumbled as she returned her glass to the table, spilling a few drops of sweet tea on the cloth place mat. "Not by choice." Voice shaking, she grabbed her napkin and dabbed at the sweet tea stain. "I didn't mean that," she whispered. "I mean, I did choose to keep the baby. I just didn't choose…" Her chin trembled and she frowned, stilling the movement as she returned the napkin to her lap. "The act of conception."

Liam froze, his fingers tightening around the spoon in his hand, the metal digging into his flesh. His eyes shot to Jessie whose smile died as she studied Mallory.

"May I ask…" Jessie said softly. "Was it your ex-husband who assaulted you?"

Mallory nodded.

Jessie moved to speak twice before finally asking, "Did it happen before or after you were divorced?"

Mallory lifted her glass to her mouth and drank deeply again before answering. "After."

Her expression grew drawn, and the color drained from her face.

Liam put his spoon down hastily and pushed his chair away from the table. "I'll leave you two alone t—"

"No!" Her tone was sharp—so sharp it made him flinch. "You don't have to leave." She jerked her chin at him, anger flashing in her eyes. "I'm not embarrassed. Or ashamed."

"As well you shouldn't be." He peered into her eyes, facing the overwhelming pain that haunted the blue depths head-on, and silently urged her to focus on his words. To believe in his sincerity. "I only meant to ensure your comfort and privacy. I'd like to hear your story if you're still okay with me being present while you tell it."

Her mouth opened and closed silently then she nodded.

"How far along are you?" Jessie asked.

"Seven months." Mallory cleared her throat. "I'm due in early March. And when I said I chose to keep the baby, I didn't mean I'd—well, I could never..." Inhaling, she rubbed her forehead. "What I meant is that I considered adoption but after a lot of prayer, I decided against it." She looked up then, her gaze moving from Jessie to Liam earnestly. "However this baby came to be, it's a part of me and I want to try to be a good mother."

Jessie reached out and covered one of Mallory's hands with her own. "And you will be." She smiled gently. "We'll do everything we can to help. I assume you came here because you'd like to relocate?"

"Yes." Mallory turned her hand over and squeezed Jessie's hand, a pleading tone entering her voice. "I need a safe place to start over. I need to relocate, get a job...begin fresh in every way just about. But I'm a hard worker and I'm willing to do whatever is needed to make a go of things. I subleased the apartment I was staying in, so I'm free of that contract, and I sold my car tonight, so I have several thousand dollars to help with putting a down payment on a new place to stay."

"And your ex-husband?" Liam bit his lip, the angry question slipping off his tongue before he could contain it. "Is that how you got that bruise on your temple? Has he attacked you again recently?"

Mallory slipped her hand free of Jessie's and touched her face. Her fingertips grazed the dark bruise on her temple then traced the swelling around her eyelid. "It's better than it was. It's not the first—or worst—time he's hit me. He was abusive during our marriage but I stayed with him for three years, hoping he'd change. We went to marriage counseling, he took an anger management class and his parents were really good people who tried to help as much as possible. The problem was just beyond them—and me— and Trevor just got worse and worse."

She placed her hands in her lap and sighed. "I filed for divorce two years ago, got my own apartment and tried to move on, but he kept showing up all the time. At my new home, at my job—he was everywhere." A cynical laugh escaped her. "It wasn't like he was heartbroken. He just couldn't stand not having control over me anymore. I tried ignoring him, warning him, reporting him—none of it worked. He always stopped short of doing anything that would get him arrested, until he r—" Her voice broke. "When I came home from work seven months ago, he was waiting by my door. He was calmer than usual—even kind—so I tried to get him to leave on my own, but he followed me inside my apartment and…"

She looked down, her hands twisting together in her lap.

Jessie leaned forward. "Afterward, did you go to the police?"

Mallory nodded. "They tried to help but it was my word against his, though. And we were married at one time so his story was that we'd briefly reconciled. I had no visible injuries or bruises—" she touched her temple and scoffed "—like this one, and he said I invited him in. It might've been different if there'd been a witness. Someone who might've heard something and come forward, but there wasn't." She squeezed her eyes shut. "I was terrified but I didn't scream." She looked at Jessie, her eyes pleading. "I don't know why I didn't scream."

"It wasn't your fault," Liam said firmly.

She looked at him, her eyes wide and pained, but resolute. "I know. In the end, I just wanted to put it behind me."

"And when you discovered you were pregnant," Jessie prompted. "What happened then?"

"Like you said, Eton's a small community." A wry smile lifted Mallory's lips. "I couldn't hide it for long and word got back to his parents three months ago. His mother asked if we could meet and I agreed."

Liam winced. After all she'd already endured, he couldn't imagine how difficult that must have been. "How did that go?"

"Trevor's mom is a good person. It was hard for her to accept what Trevor had done and to walk away from her grandchild but she did believe me and she wanted to abide by my wishes." She sighed. "She persuaded Trevor to sign away his parental rights so I could start over on my own. I was surprised when he agreed to that but I thought that'd be the end of it. And it was for a while, but a few days ago, when he found out I was moving, he showed up at my place again. He was angry—said I'd forced his hand and that this was still his child."

She gestured toward the overnight bag Liam had sat on

the floor in the living room. "The next day, I packed a few things in that bag, got in my car and left town. I stayed in a motel for a few nights and put a for sale sign on my car. Someone called yesterday, wanting to buy it, and I gave her a good deal on the condition that she'd drop me off here after taking possession of it."

"I'm glad you came," Jessie said. "How did you hear about us?"

"My preacher." Mallory issued a small smile. "I went to him for advice and he suggested I come see you. He said Hummingbird Haven had been mentioned in several churches near our area as a safe haven and he thought you could help me get established somewhere else safely."

Jessie smiled. "I'm glad he gave you our information. It was very brave of you to come."

"Yes," Liam said. "It was."

Mallory looked at them, then picked up her spoon and resumed eating. "This is wonderful, Liam," she said between bites. "Thank you." She glanced at Jessie. "For being willing to help me, too."

"Right." Jessie rubbed her hands together briskly. "Now that I have more background information and I know what resources we're working with, I can get started on making inquiries as far as placement. Do you have a particular location in mind for starting over?"

Mallory shook her head. "I'm willing to go anywhere you say is safe. But I would like to put some more distance between myself and Trevor, if possible. Some place farther away from Eton would be great."

Jessie smiled. "Then that's what I'll search for." She pushed back her chair and stood. "I'll get started right away and make a few calls tonight. You're in need of a place to stay—the farther from Eton, the better—with access to good health care and a job that's either based at home or near local transportation. Is that about right?"

"Yes." Mallory pushed her chair back, too, and moved to stand. "I can't thank you enough for helping me, Jessie."

She patted Mallory's shoulder. "You've thanked me enough. For now, stay put and eat a decent meal, then you need a good night's sleep. When you finish eating, I'll walk with you back to my place and you can stay in our guest room for the night. We'll talk strategy in the morning."

Liam stood. "What about the fireworks? Do you need me to help Holt set them up while you get Mallory settled?"

Jessie held up a hand. "No. We decided before I came here to skip the fireworks this year. The wind's too strong. Too much of a fire hazard. They'll hold in storage 'til the Fourth of July."

"I can't help but think I've put a damper on your celebration," Mallory said. "Showing up like I have, interrupting your party—and now you can't even enjoy your fireworks on account of the weather. It's not much of a New Year's Eve celebration tonight for you, is it?"

The despondent tone in her quiet voice made Liam's heart ache. What a painful journey she'd had in life and how very vulnerable she seemed. But she'd had enough strength to travel to Hummingbird Haven and there was a reason God had led her here. Of that, he was certain.

"Tonight is very much a celebration." Liam placed his hand flat on the table, as close as he could get to hers without touching. When she glanced up at him, he said softly, "It's a celebration of a new start—a new life—for you and your baby."

"I hope so," she whispered.

"I know so," he replied. "Anything is possible. All you need is faith."

She looked up at him in surprise, the longing in her expression at odds with the wounded doubt haunting her eyes.

Liam stared back at her, wanting to reassure her that her life would be different, that she would no longer have to live in fear or defend herself or her child against violence. To prove to her that although some men did aim to hurt, other men—good men—chose to protect.

In that moment, he decided that was exactly what he was going to do.

Chapter Three

Liam hadn't asked for much over the past thirty-eight years of his life but for some reason, he wanted to help Mallory find a safe place to call home. And he wanted it more than he'd wanted anything in a very long time.

"She's on her own," he said, lowering to one knee beside the bed in the guest room of Jessie's intake cabin. "For now, at least." He picked up one soft slip-on shoe from the floor, cupped his mother's left heel in his palm and slid the shoe onto her foot gently. "She's having a baby in a couple of months."

"A baby?" His mother's eyes, dazed and unfocused, strayed to the window and stared out as soft morning light slowly spread across the sky. "A real one?"

Liam smiled. "Yes, ma'am. A real one."

His mother's expression brightened. "One that cries and all?"

He slid the second shoe on her right foot. "Yep."

She clapped her hands together and laughed. "How wonderful!"

Liam sat back on his haunches and studied her expression, his smile growing at the cheerful sound she made. His mother was young—only sixty-seven—but her cognitive impairments had emerged early following a stroke and had progressed rapidly. Two years ago, she'd been an active, vibrant woman with a zest for life. Now she had difficulty performing everyday tasks independently and often forgot where she was.

Late last night, after Jessie and Mallory had left, she'd woken up and wandered off again, strolling out the front door of the cabin and into the cold night in bare feet with no sense of direction. She'd been angry when he'd caught up with her. He had walked her back inside the cabin then cleaned and rubbed her chilled feet. She'd sat upright in bed and scowled at him for over an hour until sleep overcame her.

Lately, only two things made her smile: a ten-year-old brown mare named Sugar that had recently been boarded in the stable at Pine Creek Farm, and an aloof barn cat that had taken up residence in the stable as well. Liam had named the stray Miss Priss on account of the feline's fluffy tail twitches and constant disdain for humans.

Liam chuckled softly at the memory of his mother following the stray cat around the stable, speaking sweetly and trying to pet it, while the feline turned up its nose and sashayed away. His mother had always loved animals of any kind and she still enjoyed walking to the stable every morning to feed, pet and talk to the horses and that high-and-mighty cat.

Who knows? Maybe having a new baby around to visit every morning might make her smile even more.

"Would you like that?" he asked. "Having a baby in the house?"

"Would I like it?" Her eyes, the same hazel shade as his own, returned to his face. "I'd love it." Surprise flashed through her expression. "I used to have a baby of my own once, you know? Nine pounds and seven ounces, born just after midnight. I named him Holt."

His smile slipped. "You had two babies that night, didn't you? Had a baby boy who arrived before Holt?"

She stared down at him and frowned. "No. Just Holt. I used to pick him up and rock him to sleep every time he cried."

Liam ducked his head and nodded. His mother's memory of him had faded several months ago and had yet to return, so her answer was no surprise. But the fact that she only remembered his brother's name still stung. Painfully so.

Not that it mattered. Though she could still recall Holt's name she didn't recognize his face, which did neither Holt nor Liam any good. As identical twins, they shared the same physical appearance but the similarities stopped there. Holt had always been somewhat of a thrill-seeking extrovert, a disposition that had led him to leave home at eighteen, following in their father's footsteps.

Liam winced. The memory of his father abandoning his wife and sons for another woman and a new life had been painful, but Holt's departure from Pine Creek Farm on the day they'd turned eighteen had left a hole in Liam's heart that had taken years to heal. Liam had immediately taken over management of their family farm and bed-and-breakfast, staying put in their family home after high school graduation, working back-breaking hours for years to keep the land in their mother's name and food on the table.

Even now, after reuniting with his brother and healing the rift in their family upon Holt's reemergence in his life, Liam occasionally felt the sting of resentment. Some of it was for the years of estrangement from his brother, some for the opportunities he'd missed out on in his own life as a result of staying put and taking responsibility for the family farm, and some of it—the part that shamed him the most—was for the fact that his mother, the person he'd loved and cared for his entire life, had no memory of him at all. Not even his name.

Liam didn't know who he was in her mind now. A caretaker? Friend? An annoying stranger who dragged her back indoors when she roamed, reminded to her eat and take her medicine?

There was no sure way to know.

Sighing, Liam stood and held out his hand. "It's a bit early for breakfast with Jessie and the kids but Holt always brews coffee before the break of dawn. Wanna walk up to his cabin with me? See how he's doing this morning?"

"My Holt is here?" Her expression was as surprised this morning as it had been yesterday morning and each day before when he'd delivered the same news throughout their two-week visit at Hummingbird Haven.

"Yeah." Liam took her hands in his and gently coaxed her to her feet. "He might even be waiting outside for us already. But it's cold out." He grabbed a long wool coat from the end of the bed and slipped it over her arms, one at a time, taking care to tug the material slowly over her frail arms. "You'll need all your winter gear today."

Five minutes later, with his mother bundled up in her warm coat, hat and gloves, Liam donned his own jacket and led her outside.

Holt, as Liam had guessed, was already waiting for them on the front porch, his hands thrust deep into his coat pockets, smiling wide in the morning sunlight. He'd followed the same routine every morning of their two-week stay at Hummingbird Haven for the holidays. Before the sun rose, he'd stroll down the hill from his and Jessie's cabin, lean on the porch rail of the intake cabin and wait for their mother to emerge.

Every morning, he smiled at her. But there was a heavy look in his eyes—one Liam easily recognized.

Grief.

"Morning, Mom." Holt hugged her then kissed her cheek. "I see you're up early as usual. You're on vacation. You should sleep in at least one morning."

Gayle frowned up at him. "Who are you?"

"I'm Holt. Your son." Smiling wider, he pointed at the dirt road that curved behind the intake cabin. "I'm the guy who lives up the hill a bit, just around that curve."

She blinked, her focus seeming to turn inward. "Is Miss Priss there? She needs her breakfast."

Holt glanced at Liam and lifted one eyebrow.

"Arrogant barn cat." Liam issued a wry smile. The feline, she remembered.

Holt grinned. "Oh. Unfortunately, Miss Priss isn't here. She's back at Pine Creek. But I just put on a strong pot of coffee and Jessie picked up some more of that cinnamon creamer you like." He moved closer and nudged their mother with his elbow. "So how 'bout it? Wanna take a stroll up the hill with me and Liam? Get a hot cup of joe?"

She thought it over, eyeing Holt then Liam, and sighed. "Might as well. Walks do a body good."

"That's the spirit." Holt patted her hand after she looped her arm around his extended elbow then waited as she did the same with Liam. "Cinnamon joe, here we come."

The sun was awake now. It peeked over the mountain range and stretched out its rays, the gold beams of light spearing through the canopy of evergreen trees overhead.

"It's a gorgeous morning." Holt slowed his steps to match Gayle's pace. "Colder than usual."

Liam tucked his mother's arm snugly against his and covered her gloved hand with his palm. Her steps, though slow, were steady this morning. "You warm enough, Mom?"

She nodded as she surveyed their surroundings, her gaze roving over the gritty dirt that crunched beneath their shoes then taking in the tall trees that bent in the winter breeze.

"Jessie and the kids are up," Holt said. "The boys wanted pancakes and bacon. Whatcha think, Mom? Pancakes sound good to you?"

Gayle didn't answer. Instead, she continued to study her surroundings, a small smile appearing.

"Mallory up, too?" Liam asked.

"Not yet. She was already settled in the guest room by the time I brought the kids home last night and was still in there sleeping when I left to come get y'all." He chuckled. "They had a blast at the New Year's Eve party. Ate about a pound of pizza, drank a gallon of soda then limboed and danced 'til they slap gave out."

Liam smiled. "I bet they slept good, too."

"Like rocks." Holt laughed again. "I'm surprised they got up as early as they did, but I suspect they were curious about our new guest since they didn't get a chance to meet her last night."

"Jessie mention if she'd found a place for Mallory to stay yet?"

"No. But she was working on it late into the evening. Called just about every contact we have, but she's still waiting on responses on account of the holiday and late hour."

Liam cupped Gayle's elbow, guiding her around a knotted root that protruded from the dirt path. "What about Pine Creek?"

Holt glanced at him. "Say what?"

"You heard me." Liam's neck prickled under Holt's scrutiny. He kept his gaze on the dirt path in front of them. "I could use the help and there's plenty of room."

Holt fell silent for a moment then asked, "Help with the bed-and-breakfast?"

"And Mom." Liam glanced down at her face, but she seemed uninterested in his and Holt's conversation as she continued taking in the mountain views. "I'd feel better having an extra pair of eyes and hands in the house round-the-clock rather than just for a few hours a day, which is what the home care aide's been providing."

"There's an easy fix for that. I told you Mom's welcome here anytime, for as long as you want. Jessie and I'll set the guest room up as close as we can to the room she has at the farm, and we'll take over her care. That'll give you time to—"

"Thank you," Liam said softly. "You know I appreciate the offer." He looked at Holt then, meeting his eyes over their mother's gray head. "I truly do. But she's most comfortable at the farm. Less confused. She's lived there her whole life. That land and that sassy cat are about the only things she remembers clearly anymore."

Holt sighed, his gaze straying to Gayle. "Yeah. But I miss her."

In more ways than one.

Liam rubbed his stubbled jaw with his free hand, hearing the words in his mind even though Holt hadn't said them. His brother had reunited with their mother only a few years prior to her illness occurring, and even though they'd reestablished a close, loving bond before she'd succumbed to dementia, he could imagine just how painful it was for Holt to lose her all over again.

"The farm's your home, too, Holt. You know you, Jessie

and the kids are welcome anytime. No need to call ahead, just come."

"I know." Holt lifted his chin toward the two-story cabin that drew into view as they ascended the hill. "But we're rooted here. My heart's wherever Jessie is and Hummingbird Haven is more than home to both of us. It's where God called us to do His work."

Liam smiled, his chest warming with pride. For years, Holt had worked hard to turn his life around and become a good man and now he was a loving husband and father who worked selflessly alongside Jessie to improve the lives of the women and children who sought refuge here. Not only had Holt become a good man, he was now the best man Liam knew.

"You and Jessie do a lot of good here," Liam said. "Maybe this is my chance to do the same."

"But is taking Mallory in what you really want?" Holt hesitated. "I mean, you've always stepped in for Mom and you've had more than your fair share of responsibility over the years. You'll be taking on more than just an extra pair of hands. There'll be a baby soon and the house'll be—"

"Full up," Liam said. "There'll be the baby, Mallory, Mom, guests…" He smiled. "The farm'll be lively again. Active. And Mallory and the baby will be protected and secure."

Holt fell silent for a moment then said, "From what Jessie told me, Mallory's been through a real tough time. And the women who come here with pasts like that aren't usually looking for—or wanting—a hero."

"I'm not looking to be her hero. I only want—"

"To be less lonely."

Liam stiffened.

"I'm sorry," Holt said quietly. "I don't mean that in the

wrong way or to offend you, I just…" He sighed. "All I mean is that I know how difficult things have been for you lately. How painful and scary Mom's illness is and how much you love visiting here and how much you enjoy being a great uncle to my kids. You've put your own life on hold for a lot of years to take care of Mom and the farm. That's my fault for abandoning Mom like I did years ago, and I regret that more than you know."

He's right. Liam's throat closed. He swallowed hard, ignoring the surge of grief that rose in his chest. *But he isn't completely right.* "I don't hold that against you—"

"I know. And I also know having others around is a nice distraction for you. It helps lighten the load. But bringing Mallory and her baby to the farm or filling up the house with people isn't going to take away the pain in terms of what's to come with Mom. Not to mention, what Mallory really needs right now is—"

"I only want to help. That's all. Isn't that what God wants us to do? Serve others when we can?" He met Holt's eyes, holding his gaze. "You remember how tough it was for Mom after Dad left us? Having to work and take care of us on her own? It would've been so much easier for her if she'd had a little help. Mallory's in a similar position now, and I have the resources and the opportunity she needs to rebuild her life in a safe home. If she comes to Pine Creek, she won't have to go it alone like Mom did—at least, not right off the bat."

They reached the top of the hill and Holt's cabin came into full view. Gayle's feet halted, bringing all three of them to a standstill.

Admiring the view, she said the same phrase she'd announced every morning since they'd been at Hummingbird Haven. "Gracious, what a gorgeous home!"

Liam nodded and said softly, "It's what everyone deserves. A safe place of their own to call home and put down roots. Pine Creek Farm can offer Mallory the same." He looked at Holt. "Don't you think so, Holt?"

He stared back at Liam for a moment then tugged Gayle forward into a comfortable pace, resuming their walk toward the cabin. "Yeah, well…you're gonna have to convince Jessie—and Mallory—of that."

"Are you sure about this, Liam?"

Sighing, Mallory blinked heavily and opened her eyes. Morning sunlight, pouring through sheer lace curtains into the small bedroom, casted a golden glow over the white comforter covering her. A crow cawed nearby as though it was perched high in an evergreen right outside the window.

She was in the guest room at Jessie's cabin, lying in bed, wearing a pair of flannel maternity pajamas Jessie had rounded up for her. That much she remembered—and was extremely grateful for.

It'd been dark when she'd followed Jessie down a dirt path to her home last night, but lights had glowed warmly inside the cabin when they'd arrived. Inside, framed photos of a happy family were displayed prominently with Jessie and her husband—Liam's twin, much to Mallory's surprise—smiling as brightly as the twin boys and toddler girl who were pictured with them in the photos.

Along the foyer and around the living room, children's toys and stuffed animals and a colorful blanket were strewn about in a happy way, as though Jessie and her husband encouraged their sons and daughter to play and enjoy themselves throughout the house. The guest room was bright and inviting, and the extra down pillows on the bed had fit perfectly along Mallory's swollen belly, supporting her through the first deep, peaceful night's sleep she'd had in months.

Mallory frowned, a pang of loss moving through her. When she'd married and moved into the first house of her own with Trevor, she'd been excited to make the space a warm, inviting home. Trevor, however, had dismissed her opinions outright and had chosen all of the furniture and decor himself. Throughout their marriage, he'd expected her to keep every inch of their home according to his specifications and she'd never had a space of her own. Even her side of their walk-in closet, full of only clothes that Trevor had approved of her wearing, was required to be arranged in a specific order like the rest of the rooms in the house.

Shirts were hung on plastic hangers to the right, pants in the middle and dresses on the left. Shoes, laces folded neatly over the toes, had to be stored on a wooden shoe rack, lined from right to left in order of occasion. Formal first and casual last.

Any deviation from the norm elicited punishment.

"I mean, it's a lot to take on."

That was Jessie's voice again. Muffled but still discernable, coming from the vicinity of the front porch near the bedroom window.

Mallory shoved off the comforter, rolled over onto her bottom and dangled her legs over the edge of the mattress. A familiar ache resumed in her lower back. Moaning, she rubbed the small of her back, just above her right hip, then looked down at her protruding belly where a visible movement within delivered a sharp jab at her ribs.

She winced and curled her fists into the top of the mattress, waiting for the baby to settle comfortably again inside her womb.

"I want to help her. I don't think it's a coincidence that

I was the one in that cabin when she arrived. It's as though it were planned. I can't think of a single reason why it wouldn't work."

That was Liam's voice now, sounding right outside the window. Deep and even. She recognized it immediately, her fists relaxing slightly against the mattress. It was the calmness in his tone that caught her attention. Trevor had never spoken in such a soothing way.

"I need the help as well," Liam's voice continued. "I truly do. I mean, cleaning the guest rooms for the bed-and-breakfast, boarding the horses and running the business while taking care of Mom has become almost impossible over the past few months." A heavy sigh sounded. "She's getting worse every day now. Noticeably so."

"I know," Jessie said.

Frowning, Mallory eased her bare feet to the floor and padded quietly over to the window. She slid one lace curtain back slightly, just enough to peek out at the two figures standing on the front porch. Jessie and Liam, bundled in warm coats, were both leaning against the porch rail, holding cups of hot coffee in their hands.

She hesitated and glanced back at the bed, guilt from eavesdropping prompting her to consider slipping away from the window as quietly as she'd approached.

"I could use an extra pair of hands and eyes when it comes to taking care of her," Liam continued. "She's up at all hours now. Last night, she fell asleep early and slept soundly for about three hours but not long after you and Mallory left to come here, she was up and about again." He frowned and rubbed his forehead. "She even went outside, starting walking through the woods before I woke up and noticed she was gone. If I hadn't fallen asleep on the couch and the cold air from the open door hadn't woken me…there's no telling what might've happened to her."

Curiosity got the better of Mallory. She tugged the curtain back a bit more and leaned closer to the window, pressing her uninjured temple against the cold glass. They were speaking about Liam's mother, who had been asleep when she'd first arrived the night before. He'd mentioned she wasn't well and that noises like fireworks made her uncomfortable. Could she be suffering from dementia?

"I don't know how you've handled things on your own for this long, Liam," Jessie said.

"I wanted to." His calm, even tone had changed, and his words had grown heavy.

Mallory tilted her head and squinted against the sunlight streaming over the mountains at their back for a better view of his face.

But he looked down at his boots, his muscular build and broad shoulders blocking out the sunlight, somewhat cloaking his handsome features in shadow as he dragged one hand over his stubbled jaw, then lifted his coffee mug to his lips. He drank deeply, the strong column of his throat moving as he swallowed, then he lowered his mug and cradled it in his big hands.

"I want Mom with me," he said. "In her own home where she feels safe and comfortable, for as long as possible."

"I understand," Jessie said, running a hand through her long hair. "But, Liam, there'll come a time when—"

"Yes, I know." Liam pushed off the porch rail and straightened, his tone firm again. "But we're not there yet and right now, I need extra help at home. Mallory's in need of a soft landing. I can give her that. She'll have free room and board, a better-than-average salary to help her save financially and the ability to work from home. In exchange,

I'll be able to focus on work when I need to while know-ing Mom's in capable hands. Getting work done faster on a regular basis means having free time again. Quality free time that I can spend with Mom."

Jessie looked up at him. "And the baby?"

Mallory looked down at her middle and cringed. The curve of her belly blurred as tears filled her eyes.

"I'm renovating one of the guest rooms in the main house already," Liam said. "I can easily turn it into a nursery. That way, Mallory can stay put in one place for a while after the baby's born. She'll have everything she and the baby will need, and she'll be able to continue saving for a place of her own when she's ready."

"Liam…" Jessie said quietly. "Have you considered how Mallory will respond to your offer?" She spread one arm to the side. "I mean, she's had a very traumatic history, and she was clearly uncomfortable around you last night. Not to mention, you live hours from here on an isolated farm in the middle of nowhere. I don't know that she'd take to pack-ing up and moving out to the country with a strange man."

She's got that right. Mallory dragged the back of her forearm over her wet lashes and frowned. Just the thought of moving into a house in a strange place with a strange man was enough to make her shudder. And she wasn't a charity c—

"It's not the middle of nowhere," Liam said. "It's my family home in peaceful countryside down south. It's not as cold there as it is here right now and spring'll be here before you know it. You know how beautiful it is there in the spring. Even though she'd be assuming a caretaking position, Mallory might find Mom is good company when she wants it. Outside of that, I wouldn't crowd her. I'd give her all the space and time she needs. She'd have fresh air, sunshine and room to breathe."

Mallory stilled. The benefits Liam described sounded overly generous considering the going rate for caretaking positions. She wasn't a charity case and didn't need another man bulldozing into her life! But, oh…

Room to breathe.

How wonderful that sounded.

"She may still turn you down, despite all that," Jessie said.

Liam nodded. "Maybe. But I don't think she will. She's too brave to turn down an opportunity for a fresh start out of fear."

Mallory's gaze shot to his face. He moved, his broad shoulder shifting as he lifted his face into full view of the sunlight and stared back at her, his eyes meeting hers through the window, his gaze gentle but steady.

"She made it this far on her own," he said softly. "She's strong enough to take the next step."

Mallory dropped the curtain back into place and stumbled back from the window. Gracious! How long had he known she was there?

Lifting her trembling fingers to her lips, her gaze darted around the room, taking in the clean, comfortable surroundings and the soft, rumpled bed she'd slept in so soundly. Her breathing began to slow as she turned his words over in her mind.

Fresh air, sunshine…room to breathe.

It sounded like a dream. The same kind of dream she'd had for months now. One of living a peaceful, comfortable life. Sleeping soundly at night and living her days free of fear. And his words: *All you need is faith. Take the next step…*

Those couldn't be a coincidence, could they?

She looked up at the ceiling, imagining the cold, clear sky beyond, trying to peer beyond the doubts that still clouded her mind. "Is this it? Is this the direction I should take?"

She couldn't afford another mistake. Couldn't afford to let her guard down and put her trust in another man who would hurt her or let her down...especially now.

A strong kick to her ribs made her flinch and her hands automatically reached for her belly, her fingertips brushing the firm mound before she could stop them. She closed her eyes and forced her palms to press gently against the warm swell of her belly for the briefest of moments, then she crossed the room, grabbed her coat and tugged it on.

Holt's deep voice, the sounds of children's laughter and the clink of utensils emerged from the kitchen as she walked down the hallway, but she didn't stop. Instead, she kept moving, taking one step after another in her bare feet until she reached the front door, opened it and stepped out onto the porch.

"Do you promise?" She stood there, clutching her coat together over the bulge of her belly, as her eyes met Liam's, urging him to answer.

He hesitated, glancing briefly at Jessie, who stared at them with surprise, before returning his attention back to her. "Promise what?"

"That there'll be fresh air, sunshine and room to breathe." Mallory shivered as a cold wind rolled over the porch and her toes grew numb against the wood planks. "That you won't crowd me? That you're offering me a legitimate care-taking job where I can earn my keep and that I won't be seen—or treated—like a charity case?"

He nodded, glancing down at her bare feet before meeting her eyes again. "I promise. Pine Creek's a safe place where you can start over in whatever way you choose."

She looked at Jessie, her heart pounding heavily as she searched the other woman's expression. "I know you're married to his brother and that you'll probably be biased, but I've also been told that you're honest—almost to a fault." She licked her lips, the tender skin already drying in the winter wind. "Can I trust him?"

Jessie smiled. "Yes, Mallory. You can trust him."

"Or..." Mallory fell silent then dragged in a trembling breath and held out her hand. "I can at least try."

Liam stared at her hand as it dipped slightly beneath a strong push of frigid wind. Then he set his coffee mug on the porch rail, moved closer and slowly closed his hand around hers.

Mallory tried to adjust to the feel of his big hand enveloping hers, forcing herself to focus on the warmth of his palm against her cold skin rather than the sight of his muscular wrist. "Th-thank you for your kind offer, Liam. I accept."

"You're welcome, Mallory," he said softly.

She stood there, his hand covering hers, while a strong surge of fear and uncertainty urged her to break free and run. But this stranger—this man—standing in front of her thought she was brave...something she'd never truly felt before in her life. She hoped, with every fiber of her being, that he was right.

Chapter Four

Gayle Williams was loved.

"And look at that right there." Gayle, shifting in the front passenger seat of Liam's truck, pointed at a snowcapped mountain in the distance. "That's snow, isn't it, young man?"

Liam's big hands moved over the steering wheel as he navigated a sharp curve in the road. "Yes, ma'am. January's much colder up here than back home. Before long, that snow'll make its way down the mountain and Holt's yard will be covered in it."

Gayle shivered. "Oh. I hope he has a coat."

Liam nodded. "He does."

"And gloves?" she asked.

"Yes, ma'am."

"And a hat?"

"Yes, ma'am."

"And…" Gayle's attention drifted to the other side of the winding road and she gasped. "Look at those trees! So very tall. Right to the sky, wouldn't you say, young man?"

Liam nodded. "Yes, ma'am. Right to the sky."

She patted one of his hands as it moved over the steering wheel. "Take care, sir. You're not going too fast, are you?"

"No, ma'am."

"These curves are sneaky," she said. "You're being careful, aren't you?"

"Yes, ma'am."

"I hope so," she said. "My Miss Priss is hungry and we need to feed her first thing when we arrive. You remember that, don't you?"

A muscle ticked in Liam's strong jaw but his expression remained patient in the rearview mirror as he recited his answer. "Yes, ma'am."

Mallory smiled. Seated in the back seat of the extended cab, she'd listened to Liam's conversation with his mother for over twenty minutes now, ever since they'd left Hummingbird Haven and begun the long drive down to Pine Creek Farm. Though she really couldn't call it a conversation since the vast majority of the talking had definitely been one-sided.

Gayle had spoken almost nonstop since they'd left Jessie's place, asking dozens of questions about the landscape—repeating many of them more than once—and frequently cautioning Liam as he drove, never once referring to him by his name.

It'd been clear to Mallory yesterday, after accepting Liam's job offer and meeting his mother, that Gayle had no memory of Liam. Gayle had looked at Liam the same way she'd looked at Mallory when Liam had introduced them to each other—with the same curious gaze of interest in a stranger.

Having lost her parents at a young age, Mallory knew how painful the loss was but could only imagine how difficult it must be for Liam to see, talk to and care for his mother every day, knowing she no longer knew him. And today, after they'd said goodbye to Jessie and her family, settled into the truck and started the journey to Pine Creek, Gayle had continuously referred to Liam as *young man* or *sir*, an impersonal reference Mallory knew must hurt him.

But despite this, Liam had remained patient, polite and kind throughout every mile they'd traveled.

"Who's Miss Priss?" Mallory asked.

Liam met her eyes in the rearview mirror, one corner of his mouth lifting in wry amusement. "A stray cat."

"*My* cat." Gayle shimmied in her seat, reached back and patted Mallory's knee. "She's just beautiful—has thick, striped fur and long, luxurious whiskers." Her voice lowered to a whisper. "Miss Priss doesn't care for this gentleman next to me. She doesn't take to him at all."

"She doesn't take to anyone," Liam said, lifting one blond brow as he glanced at Mallory in the rearview mirror. "Gives Mom a run for her money every time she tries to pet it, turns her nose up at the food I give her half the time and claws my shins every time I walk in the stable. That cat's the most uppity creature I've ever run across."

"Well, now." Gayle faced forward again, tidied the collar of her thick coat then folded her gloved hands in her lap. "That wasn't a very nice thing to say. It was quite rude, actually. I think you owe Miss Priss an apology."

Liam broke then. Rolling his eyes, he leaned his head to one side and issued a long-suffering sigh.

"And now..." Gayle said, lifting her chin. "You owe me an apology, too. You should never roll your eyes at someone whether you disagree with them or not. It's disrespectful. Didn't your mother teach you that, young man?"

Liam looked at his mother. He moved to speak then stopped before facing the road ahead and reciting, "Yes, ma'am. I apologize for offending you."

Gayle nodded. "Accepted. And you'll apologize to Miss Priss?"

The muscle in Liam's jaw ticked again. "Yes, ma'am."

"Good." Gayle smiled and rubbed her hands together. "I

can't wait until we get to the farm." She frowned. "These curves are sneaky. You're being careful, aren't you, young man?"

The one-sided conversation began again, interrupted only by Liam's refrain of "Yes, ma'am."

Mallory smiled wider. Liam definitely loved his mother.

She settled back in her seat, stretched her legs as far as they could go in the back of the extended cab—which was much roomier than she'd anticipated—and looked out the window at the scenery as it passed.

Liam was making good time. From what he'd told her yesterday, Pine Creek Farm was a little more than three hours away from Hummingbird Haven. There had been little traffic on the highway thus far, and the Blue Ridge Mountain ranges soon gave way to gentler slopes and hills. The light layers of snowfall were soon behind them and the sun's rays grew stronger as they traveled, lending extra warmth to the truck's cab, creating a cozy cocoon.

Her eyes grew heavy and she blinked, trying to envision the farm Liam had described. As inviting as Jessie's guest bed had been, it had been difficult to sleep last night, knowing that the journey to Pine Creek Farm would begin today. She'd spent most of the night tossing and turning, imagining how Liam's family home might appear based off how he'd described it.

Peaceful countryside. Fresh air, room to breathe. A main house with multiple guest rooms.

It sounded so wonderful. Like a pleasant gathering place. It sounded like…a home. Something she hadn't had in a very long time.

A yawn overtook her and she wiped her watery eyes, refocusing on the passing landscape as Gayle continued asking Liam questions he'd already answered ten miles back.

In the end, it didn't matter if the place didn't live up to Liam's hype. Whatever Pine Creek Farm turned out to be, it had to be better than what she'd left behind. Any place far removed from Trevor that offered her a way to make a living and start her life over was a step in the right direction.

But, oh, she hoped it turned out to be exactly as Liam had described. *Peaceful countryside. Fresh air, room to breathe...*

"Mallory?" Something big and warm nudged her shoulder gently. "Mallory, we're here."

Her eyes popped open, and she looked up at Liam as he stood beside the open door of the truck's cab, then glanced down. His palm was curved lightly around her shoulder.

He removed it and stepped back. "I'm sorry. I hated to wake you but it's too cold to nap out here." He grinned. "I promise you our guest room will be more comfortable than the truck."

The sun was much lower in the sky than before and the truck was parked at the end of a long, paved driveway, surrounded by open fields.

Fumbling, she unbuckled her seat belt and scrambled upright. "I missed it."

"Missed what?"

"Everything." Rubbing her eyes, she shifted her legs to the side and scooted closer to the open door. "The ride into Pine Creek, the drive up to the farm, everything. I wanted to see it all when we—"

"Hey," he said softly. "Slow down. The farm's not going anywhere and there's still some sunlight left. I can show you around a bit before we go in, if you'd like. But please be careful getting out of the truck. It's a steep drop and it'd be easy for the two of you to take a tumble."

She frowned. The two of...?

Oh.

She looked down at the bulge of her belly, her cheeks heating.

"Here." Liam's hand lifted into her line of vision. "I'll help you down, if you'd like?"

She drew in a deep breath and placed her hand in his, leaning on it as she slid out of the truck's cab and stood on the paved driveway. "Thank you."

"Sure thing." He released her hand as soon as she was steady on her feet then shut the door behind her. "Did you have enough room back there? I was hoping you'd take me up on my offer to sit up front because the seats back there are a bit tight."

"It was fine." She tugged the hood of her jacket onto her head, blocking the wind's chill against her ears. "I had plenty of room and I felt better knowing Mrs. Gayle's routine wasn't changed on account of me joining you."

"Thank you for thinking of her. She's anxious to—"

"Excuse me, young man!" Gayle stood at the front of the truck, bundled up in a warm coat and hat, wringing her gloved hands together with an excited expression. "Miss Priss is hungry and I can't wait on y'all forever."

He smiled. "Yes, ma'am." He glanced at Mallory, his smile growing. "As I was saying, she's anxious to introduce you to Miss Priss. And I gotta say, better you than me. I've had my fill of that cat."

Mallory smiled back. "And from what I hear, you owe it an apology."

He winked. "So it seems."

There was a dimple—a small one—in his left cheek. It was barely visible but appeared when he smiled wide as he did now. Liam Williams, it seemed, could very easily be perceived as charming…if a woman allowed herself to notice that sort of thing.

Trevor had been charming, too. In the beginning.

She looked away and shoved her hands into the pockets of her coat. "You said you'd show me around a little before we go inside?"

"Of course. Mom's anxious to see that cat so we'll visit the stable first. It's this way."

She waited, her eyes still staring at the pavement beneath her shoes, until his heavy steps receded then lifted her head and followed, deliberately lagging behind a few paces.

Liam looked over his shoulder as he walked, his hazel eyes concerned as they studied her face. "You all right back there?"

"Yeah. Just taking in the view." She turned her head and surveyed their surroundings, her steps slowing even more at the sight of the winding driveway lined with beautiful white fencing that seemed to go on for miles. "2971 Magnolia Lane."

"What's that?" Liam asked.

"Magnolia Lane," Mallory said louder. "That was the address on your license, right?" She pointed at dozens of trees with bare branches that had been planted in perfect lines along the white fencing. "Are those magnolia trees?"

Liam nodded. "You've got a good memory. And yeah, those are magnolias. They bloom every year sometime in March. Mom helped my grandfather plant those when she was a little girl. They're her favorite part of spring."

"I bet." When blooming, they were probably a sight to behold. That was something she could look forward to. "There are so many fields. How much land is yours?"

"Everything you can see and then some." Liam cupped Gayle's elbow as she stepped off the paved driveway and onto the dormant grass, then walked toward a large white stable with a black roof. "Around seventy acres in all. We board horses and give trail rides, so the extra acreage comes in handy."

"How many horses do you have?" she asked as they drew closer to the stable.

"Nine right now," Liam said, opening the stable door and stepping back to allow Gayle to enter first. "Our stalls are full and I'm looking into investing in another stable, but that depends on this year's revenue."

"Do you grow crops or is this strictly a horse farm?"

"We have a substantial vegetable garden and sell those crops locally, but the horse side of the business took off a few years ago, so we've gravitated toward that. If I've learned anything from running this business over the years, it's that change is the only constant and the best thing to do is welcome it." He gestured for her to enter. "The stable's newly renovated. There are nine stalls, two wash-and-groom stalls, a tack-and-grain room and an office. Take a look around."

She walked inside and strolled slowly down the center of the stable. The floors were comprised of gray rubber pavers and the ceiling and stalls were white with black trim. Tall, healthy horses of various colors stood in each stall and the air was comfortably warm.

"It's beautiful," she said. "And squeaky-clean. How do you manage that with white stalls?"

He grinned. "Lots of washing and scrubbing. We've got a small—but great—crew of hands that do the bulk of the work. Takes extra pay and effort to keep everything sparkly but it's worth it to keep the bed-and-breakfast side of the business going. When our guests visit, they're looking for a peaceful, country retreat and this type of appealing atmosphere lends itself to that. We try to make Pine Creek Farm feel like a home away from home for them."

Mallory nodded. "It's certainly impressive." She walked farther into the stable, scanning the horses in each stall. "Are any of these horses yours?"

"Three of them, yeah. I lead guests on trail rides around the property with them." He eased around her and walked toward the last stall on the left. "Sugar's a favorite. She's a sweetheart. I think you'll like her the b—"

His voice broke and a strangled growl left his throat as a big ball of striped fur wrapped around his boot and four sets of claws dug into his jean-clad shin. He lifted his right leg and shook his foot, but the more Liam shook his leg, the more the cat writhed on his shin and boot.

"Get off, cat!" Liam said.

A yelp burst from his mouth and Mallory grinned. It was a sight—this big man balancing on one leg, at the mercy of a cat.

"Miss Priss!" Gayle, who'd been searching the stable for the cat, clapped her hands together and grinned. "See—all that thick fur and long whiskers. I told you Miss Priss was beautiful. She's telling us hello, aren't you, sweetie?"

"Mom." Liam winced and kicked harder. "Her claws are so deep, she's hitting bone."

Mallory stilled, her smile dissipating and her heart pounding in her ears. Her hands lifted automatically. Liam was taller than Trevor—probably stronger, too—and the cat was so small. The deeper his frown grew, the harder his muscular leg jerked. One hefty kick of his leg, a bit stronger than before, and the cat's grip might dislodge, causing it to sail through the air and slam into the hard wood of a stall.

The cat's claws dug deeper as it released a low, panicked moan.

Let go. Trevor's voice hissed through her mind. The memory caught her off-guard, as usual. It burst forth, stealing an otherwise light-hearted moment—twisting it into something dark and sinister.

She could still feel the muscles of his forearm flex beneath her fingers as she'd tried to loosen his vicious grip on her hair. Even her scalp stung at the memory. His weight had been so heavy—too heavy to move.

Let go, or it'll be worse.

She opened her mouth but no sound emerged, a high-pitched plea lodging in her throat.

"Okay, okay." Liam stopped kicking his leg and lowered his boot to the floor. "I get it—you're scared, huh?" His voice grew quiet as he spoke to the cat, his words slow and tone low. "Hang out for a while. Have a go at the other leg, too, if you'd like."

After a few moments of stillness, the cat's tense posture relaxed and it inched back down Liam's shin and onto his boot, blinking up at him with wide green eyes.

"Good girl." Liam bent and eased his hand, palm upward, towards the cat's nose. "I'm not so bad, you know. You might like me if you give me a chance, huh?"

The cat stared, unblinking, at his hand then sprang off Liam's boot and darted away, scurrying out of the stable.

"Now look what you've done." Gayle straightened and put her hands on her hips. "You've scared her."

"I scared her?" Mouth twitching, Liam pressed his palm to the center of his wide chest. "*I* scared *her*?"

Gayle walked out of the stable, frowning at him over her shoulder. "She's hungry. But I can't feed her now since you ran her off."

Liam shook his head as Gayle left, calling after her, "She won't go hungry. The hands have fed that ornery cat every day since we left. Believe me, they've called me more than once to complain about it." Chuckling, Liam rubbed his injured shin then glanced at Mallory. His smile slowly faded as he studied her face and hands. "Mallory?"

She blinked and lowered her hands to her sides, eyeing his leg as her heart rate slowed. Her cheeks burned and she shoved her hands in her pockets to keep from covering them. "Are you okay?" Could he hear the awkward tension in her voice? "I don't see any blood."

"I'm fine," he said softly, still studying her expression. "The jeans kept her from maiming me." He shrugged. "I have no idea why that cat has such an affinity for attacking me but she does it every time I walk in here, so I should be used to it by now."

Mouth dry, she swallowed hard. "You held your own, at least."

"I guess." A small, uncertain smile returned to his face and he asked gently, "Mind if we put off meeting Sugar 'til later? My pride's taken a hit and if I don't go after Mom soon, there's no telling where she'll get off to."

Mallory nodded. "Of course."

He left the stable and she followed on stiff legs, staying a pace behind.

Sure enough, Gayle had wandered off toward the magnolia tree–lined driveway, her long gray hair billowing behind her in the winter wind. Liam caught up to her though and before long, he'd ushered her to the main house, which turned out to be a white two-story with a wraparound porch. After Gayle sat on the couch in the living room, Liam picked up a quilt that lay on the back of a recliner, draped it over her legs then turned on the TV.

"You okay here while I show Mallory around?" he asked.

Gayle focused on the TV program, her eyes growing heavy.

Liam smiled. "We'll be back soon, Mom." He joined Mallory in the foyer. "Kitchen's through here." He led the way past a large dining room and into a large kitchen with an island and stainless steel appliances. "Fridge is always stocked with fresh fruit and vegetables and there are several casseroles in the freezer that can be popped in the oven and ready to eat in a half hour. You're welcome to anything you like and if you want something that's not there, just let me know and I'll get it for you."

"You do all the cooking yourself?" Mallory asked.

"Yeah," he said. "But the frozen casseroles are dropped off once every other week by Pam Marshall. She heads up a ladies' group at our church. They like to visit Mom and always bring a couple dishes when they come."

Mallory smiled. "That's nice of them."

"Yeah. You'd like Pam. She's real down-to-earth." He stepped back and motioned for her to join him. "Follow me. I'll show you the guest rooms then we'll go upstairs and see your room."

Downstairs, there were four guest rooms. Two contained king-size beds and two queen beds were in the others. One bathroom with a large walk-in shower joined the two guest rooms on the left side of the hall and a second bathroom with a smaller shower and large garden tub joined the other two guest rooms. All rooms had floor-to-ceiling windows with spectacular views of the expansive fields or stable and paddocks. Liam also informed her that there were three small guesthouses on the property, each with a small bedroom, kitchen and bathroom that guests booked for more private visits.

Upstairs, there were three rooms and two bathrooms.

The largest room, directly opposite the stairway, belonged to Gayle. A room to the left of the stairs was empty save for a mahogany dresser covered with clear plastic.

"This used to be my room but I'm renovating it and staying downstairs now," Holt said. "I'd planned to turn it into another guest room at some point but I think it'd be a perfect location for your nursery."

Mallory frowned. "Oh, please don't change your plans on my account. I don't want to inconvenience y—"

"Not at all." He smiled. "From this point forward, everything upstairs belongs to you and Mom." He walked across the landing and opened the door to another room. "This one's yours."

She joined him then walked into the room, glancing around. There was a large queen-size bed decorated with fluffy pillows and a handwoven quilt in the center of the room, and floor-to-ceiling windows were opposite, offering another stunning view of the property—this time of the front yard and fenced driveway. There was an en suite bathroom as well.

"Do you like it?" he asked.

She stood with her back to him, motionless for a moment, admiring the comfortable bed, large dresser and walk-in closet. "This is for me?"

"Yes."

"All of it?"

"Yes." He fell silent then added, "I thought it'd be easier for you to help Mom at night if you were next door to her room. And she gets up a lot at night, so it'll be easier for you to hear her moving about. If the bedding's not comfortable, we've got a closet full of comforter sets downstairs you can choose from and if you don't like anything there, we can shop in town for whatever you want. If you don't like the way the sun hits in the morning, we can get new curtains or rearrange the furniture however you want."

"I… I can change it?"

"Yes," he said. "In whatever way you'd like. And—" he gestured toward her middle "—if the stairs become too much for you, we'll just switch things up. I'll move back upstairs and you can choose a room downstairs instead."

This room was hers. A space all her own. To do with as she pleased.

"If you don't like it," he said hesitantly, "I can—"

"No." She faced him then, seeking his eyes, hoping he could glimpse in hers at least a fraction of the gratitude that swelled within her. It flooded her heart and spilled onto her lower lashes. "I love it."

He smiled, tenderness in his eyes, and the sight of it filled her heart even more. "Good." Clearing his throat, he walked to the door then said as he left, "I'll bring up your bag so you can settle in."

Mallory stood there, listening as his heavy steps descended the stairs, then walked across the room and sat on the bed. Outside the wide windows, the sun began to set, dipping low against the horizon, painting the sky a soft pink, and—despite the winter chill outdoors—flooded the room with a warm glow. It was quiet here. Peaceful and calm. She closed her eyes and warm tears poured over her cheeks.

Liam leaned back, closed his eyes and sighed.

Some years ago, behind the main house at Pine Creek Farm, he'd built a stone firepit and patio. The space had become his favorite place on the farm. It was serene, sitting out here under the starry night sky, a fire blazing and fields stretching out as far as the eye could see. But it wasn't the starlight, flicker of flame or glow of the winter moon that inspired such a peaceful feeling within his heart.

It was the fact that out here, with nothing separating him from the sprawling heavens above his head and hard earth below his boots, he felt closest to God. There was something about it—the fresh, open air between his heart and the heavens above—that made him feel as though God heard his prayers more clearly.

And, more importantly, he could sometimes hear God more clearly.

For the past hour, he'd sat out here by the fire, sprawled in an Adirondack chair, staring at the stars above, asking God for guidance on how to help Mallory.

Hours earlier, after he'd shown Mallory to her room, he'd gone to his truck, unloaded his, Gayle's and Mallory's bags and carried them inside the house. He'd taken Mallory's overnight bag upstairs to her room, eager to help her settle in. But when he'd arrived, she'd been sitting on the edge of the bed, her hands flat on the mattress, her eyes closed and tears streaming down her cheeks. Unaware of his presence, she'd remained motionless and pensive as though in silent prayer or deep self-reflection.

Either way, he'd been hesitant to interrupt her. He'd placed her overnight bag on the floor just outside the open door and returned downstairs, taking quiet steps to avoid distracting her. He'd gone about his routine chores as usual, checking on the horses in the stable, paying various invoices online to vendors in his office and answering inquiries related to guest reservations for spring via email. Prospects looked good for Pine Creek Farm. As it stood, he'd booked visitors for all three guesthouses on the property from the day the bed-and-breakfast opened for the spring season until the last day of summer. If the fall season stayed as busy, Pine Creek Farm's bed-and-breakfast would generate more revenue this year than in the past two years, and with Mallory caring for his mom, he'd be able to offer an additional trail ride to guests each day, garnering more income.

Pleased at the good news, he'd returned to the main house and checked on his mom, who'd fallen asleep on the living room couch, then walked to the kitchen—a pep of cautious optimism in his step—and began cooking dinner.

Throughout it all, Mallory had not emerged from her room. But sometime later, when the rich aroma of lasagna began to waft around the house, she'd emerged from upstairs and walked into the kitchen, tears gone and a polite smile on her face as she asked if she could help him prepare the meal.

She'd set the table while he'd baked the garlic bread and by the time dinner was ready, Mallory had woken Gayle, assisted her to the dining room table and had made sure she was seated with a full glass of sweet tea before taking her own seat at the table.

The meal had been pleasant. Gayle had asked several questions about how Liam had prepared the lasagna and had complimented his culinary skills—something she used to do often but had done less as of late. Mallory had thanked him again for her room, telling him how much she liked it, and had asked several more questions about the guesthouses, the grounds and the schedule she would undertake when caring for Gayle.

He'd filled her in on his mom's most pressing needs—Gayle had briefly argued with him on a few points—and soon, he and Mallory had created a schedule with which his mom begrudgingly agreed. Mallory would serve as a live-in caretaker and companion throughout the day. She'd help his mom dress and bathe, prepare and ensure his mom ate healthy meals and snacks on a consistent basis, and stay close at hand in case his mom wandered off.

As expected, he'd earned a scowl from his mom at the mention of her wandering and "needing a babysitter," as she'd dubbed it. And she'd reminded him, in no uncertain terms, how she felt about him.

"You may be handsome," Gayle had said, "but you're annoying."

Liam's face had heated and a soft laugh had escaped Mallory. She'd tried to hide it, ducking her head and taking another bite of lasagna, but he'd noticed, and the sound of it had made him smile.

In the quiet lull between conversations, they'd eaten in comfortable silence and Liam had glanced at Mallory occasionally, hoping she wouldn't notice him scrutinizing her expression as he'd searched for a glimpse of the distress he'd seen in her eyes earlier in the stable.

He'd scared her. Of that, he was certain.

It had been unfortunate that the cat had attacked him the moment they'd arrived at the stable, but not unexpected— Miss Priss had made a habit of such a thing. But for some reason, the event had affected Mallory in a much different way than it had him or Gayle. Instead of his irritation or his mom's cheery indulgence of the cat's antics, Mallory had looked terrified. Her hands had lifted in front of her, as though shielding herself from unseen danger, and an expression of terror had appeared on her face.

The fear in her eyes had struck a deep chord of concern within him.

He closed his eyes tighter and leaned his head back against the chair's headrest. His stomach churned at the thought of what she may have endured at the hands of her ex-husband, and he could only guess at the depths of pain she hid…and the fear she probably carried for men, in general. He'd wanted to reassure her that she was safe at Pine Creek Farm…and safe with him.

At the time, he'd fumbled the moment, unsure of what to say or how to approach her. And when he'd called her name, she'd quickly redirected the conversation back to the cat's antics. He'd followed her lead, had not asked any more questions and had carried on with the tour of the farm. But after seeing her sit motionless on the bed in her room with tears streaming down her cheeks, he'd been unable to shake the urgent need to find a way to connect with her. To assure her that she could share her fears, thoughts and emotions with him without judgment. That, somehow, he could find a way to help.

Women with pasts like that aren't usually looking for— or wanting—a hero.

Liam opened his eyes as he recalled the comment Holt made during their talk at Hummingbird Haven. He'd resented the sentiment as soon as his brother had made it, but at the moment—and to an extent, even back then—he also wondered exactly how true it was.

Was that what was driving him to seek a closer connection to Mallory? Was he trying to be her hero rather than simply serve her in a time of need?

He hoped not. Helping Mallory shouldn't be about him or his own wants, it should be about—

"Mind if I join you?"

He sat upright then stood as Mallory strolled across the stone patio and stopped beside the empty Adirondack chair beside him. "Of course." He gestured toward the empty chair. "Please have a seat."

"Your mom's fast asleep," she said, placing her hands

on the armrests of the chair and easing into a seated position. She was wearing her long coat, and when she settled in the chair, it pulled across her middle, emphasizing her swollen belly. "I think she's getting used to me." A small smile curved her lips. "She let me sit with her for a while after she got in bed. She asked a dozen questions about me—what's my name, where am I from—and was in the middle of asking another when she fell asleep."

Liam laughed then sat back down in his chair. "Did she ask you to read to her?"

"Ephesians, chapter two." She smiled wider, her eyes teasing. "She said she liked my voice better than yours."

Liam laughed again and leaned back in his chair, stretching out his legs. "Thank you for volunteering to get her settled tonight. And for loading the dishwasher. I didn't expect you to hit the ground running the moment you arrived, but I have to say, it was nice to eat a good supper then come out here and relax while my stomach settled instead of jumping to the next task."

"That's why I'm here," she said. "It's my job. I'm happy to help however I can and the sooner Gayle and I get to know each other, the better we'll get along."

Liam nodded. "Well, I appreciated it. More than you know." He held his hands out, absorbing the warmth from the fire. "Are you warm enough? I could grab a blanket for you if—"

"No, thank you. I'm good."

They fell quiet for a few minutes, watching the flames flicker against the backdrop of the night sky and listening to the crackle and pop of wood as it burned. He snuck a couple glances in her direction, but she had her hood on and the bulky material obscured her face.

"Why are you helping me?"

Liam stilled. Her soft voice seemed to echo into the cold night air surrounding them. He moved to speak then hesitated before answering. "Because it's the right thing to do."

He wasn't sure why, but the weight of disappointment settled over his chest as he said the words aloud.

"I'm sorry for the way I've..." Her voice trailed away and she fell silent again.

He listened to the fire crackle for a few moments then prompted, "For the way you...?"

Her coat rustled and he looked in her direction, his gaze meeting hers as she looked at him earnestly.

"I have a lot of bad memories," she said. "And I have no control over when they come." She blinked rapidly and lowered her gaze, her cheeks flushing beneath the glow of the fire. "It's embarrassing, but...it just is."

One of his hands lifted, reaching toward hers, but he stopped the movement and gripped the armrest of his chair. "You have nothing to be embarrassed about. I'm only sorry for what you've been through."

She met his gaze, her eyes searching his, then turned away and faced the fire. Her hood hid her face again.

"Have you...?" He shifted awkwardly in his seat. "Have you spoken to someone? About the memories, I mean?"

Her hood shifted as she nodded. "It just takes time. A lot of work." She sighed. "And a lot of prayer."

Liam looked at the fire, too, watching the flames spit embers into the sky. They floated up, small red flashes amid the velvet night sky and sparkling stars. "You remember the ladies' group I mentioned? The one from my church?" At her nod, he added, "They meet often and Pam Marshall's a great leader. And a great listener. I could introduce you to her, if you'd like?"

"Yes. I'd like that very much." Voice strained, she curled

her fingers around the armrests of her chair. "And I... I have another favor to ask, please?"

"Of course. Anything."

Her coat rustled and he turned his head, meeting her gaze again. "Before we left Hummingbird Haven, Jessie made an appointment for me to see a doctor in Pine Creek." She briefly motioned toward her belly. "For a checkup, you know? My appointment's tomorrow but I don't know how to get there." She laughed, her mouth twisting. "And I don't have a car anymore."

"Not a problem," he said. "I'll drive you into town tomorrow."

"I need to go by the bank, too, please. I'd like to open an account with the money I made from selling my car, if you can spare the time?"

He smiled. "Not a problem. The bank's right around the corner from the health clinic and a coffee shop's nearby. Mom loves her lattes and always enjoys going into town. We'll help you check in for your appointment then grab a coffee and come back and pick you up." He winced. "Although... Mom likes to shop in the craft store next to the coffee shop, so if we run a little behind getting back to the clinic, don't worry. It'll depend on how bossy she gets when I tell her it's time to leave."

Her smile returned. It transformed her expression, brightening her eyes and easing the tense lines that bracketed her mouth. A brief glimpse of the happy, carefree woman he suspected she might've once been.

He wished he could give her that. Make her smile forever.

"She's definitely got a stubborn streak," she said, laughing. "But I think she's earned it."

She turned away and adjusted the hood on her head. Silence fell between them, save for the crackle of the fire and the whistle of winter wind as it swept over the open fields surrounding them.

"I was wrong," she whispered.

Liam glanced at her again but was unable to see her face. "About what?"

"It's not quiet here. Not at all," she said softly. "You hear that? The chorus of the fire and the wind? Even the stars seem to whisper."

He closed his eyes again and a tender longing spread through his heart. One that urged him to imagine what it might be like to enjoy each peaceful evening out here by the firepit beneath the stars with a woman he loved by his side. And how it might feel to be loved by her in return. "Yes."

"It's like a peaceful song," she said. "The most beautiful one I've ever heard."

Chapter Five

The next morning, Mallory stood, legs trembling, beside Liam at the check-in desk inside a health clinic within the town limits of Pine Creek.

"Mallory Kent, right?" The receptionist, a young blonde with kind eyes and a bright smile, picked up the clipboard that lay on the desk, eyed Mallory's signature then nodded with satisfaction. "Jessie Alden called us yesterday to remind us that you'd be coming today. She asked Dr. Harper to take great care of you."

Mallory tried to smile but her mouth trembled. Instead, she shoved her clammy hands into the pockets of her coat and nodded in return. "Jessie told me Dr. Harper was the best obstetrician in Pine Creek."

"One of only two obstetricians," the receptionist said, giggling. "Not that that makes her any less of the best. Her primary practice is in Dalton—that's about an hour from here—but she and Dr. Martin Zendall, our other visiting obstetrician, come to Pine Creek once a month to take care of local patients. Being a rural town, Pine Creek doesn't have the population to serve a full-time obstetrician and we're grateful to have them."

Mallory released a small sigh of relief, thanking Jessie silently in her head again for having the compassionate foresight to arrange the appointment with the female physician. Being cared for by a female doctor rather than a male wouldn't silence the turmoil inside her at the thought of being examined, but it would at least help.

"All I need is your state-issued ID and health insurance card, please," the receptionist said, holding out her hand. "Then I'll have you fill out a new patient packet."

Mallory dug around in her coat pocket and withdrew her license, but hesitated before handing it over. "I have my ID, but I don't have any insur—"

"I'll be serving as the guarantor for Mallory's account," Liam said. "Is there a place for me to write down my information so you can bill me for the visits?"

The receptionist's eyes widened with surprise as she smiled at Liam. "Of course, Liam." The receptionist picked up another clipboard with several sheets of paper attached, removed one page and handed it to him. "Here's the payment form from the new patient packet. You can jot down your information there, although I already know where to find you." She winked. "My sister and brother-in-law are bringing their kids for a visit on spring break. I told them they better get with you quick if they want to book one of the guesthouses at Pine Creek Farm again."

Liam smiled. "That's a good idea. We've gotten a lot of reservations for spring already." He tapped the paper in his hand. "Mallory's my newest employee. She's caring for my mom and helping with the bed-and-breakfast."

The receptionist smiled at Mallory. "How wonderful! Pine Creek Farm is so beautiful in the spring! You'll love it."

"Thank you," Liam said. "And you'll be sure to send any invoices for Mallory's care to me?"

The receptionist turned to a desktop computer and began

typing on the keyboard. "I'll make a note of it in the system now."

Mallory reached for the paper. "Liam, you don't have to do that—"

He pressed the paper to his chest and grabbed a pen from the desk. "I know. But we haven't discussed health benefits yet so consider it part of your salary." He smiled. "I'll get this filled out and everything'll be taken care of. You just focus on taking care of yourself."

Mallory shook her head. "But, Liam—"

"Oh, magazines!" Gayle, who'd been strolling around the waiting room, picked up a garden magazine and sat down in a comfortable chair by the window. "Now, if I just had a cup of coffee, I'd be set."

"Welp," Liam said, "that's my cue. After I fill this out, I'll take Mom next door to the coffee shop, grab a latte then we'll come back to pick you up." His eyes, concerned, narrowed as he studied her face. "Unless you'd like us to stay and wait for you here?"

Mallory bit her lip, wanting to ask him to stay. But why, she didn't know. So far, she'd attended all her checkups alone and this one was no different.

Only, it had felt different walking into this clinic today, chatting with the receptionist and filling out paperwork with Liam by her side. She'd felt less alone—almost as though she had a friend or teammate, cheering her on and wishing her well, ready to catch her if she were to fall. And looking at him now, studying the concern in his eyes and his patient expression, she found herself admiring his selflessness and generosity all the more.

So far, Liam was nothing like Trevor. Liam had been so calm and kind. So caring and understanding. If he were genuine—if he didn't turn out to be too good to be true—

any woman would be lucky to have a man like him as a friend.

But Liam wasn't aiming to be her friend, was he? And this baby wasn't his responsibility. What was it he'd said last night by the fire? About why he decided to help her?

Because it's the right thing to do. Nothing more, nothing less.

She was a good deed for a good man.

"No." She forced the word out between stiff lips, wanting to take it back as soon as she said it. "I'm okay. Thank you."

The concern in Liam's eyes deepened.

A door beside the check-in desk opened and a middle-aged woman with glasses and a topknot called out, "Mallory Kent?"

"I…" Mallory dragged her hands from her pockets and rubbed her clammy palms down the side of her pants. "I'm Mallory Kent."

The woman smiled and propped the door open a bit further. "Nice to meet you, Mallory. I'm Dr. Harper. Would you like to come on back and get started?"

Hesitating, Mallory glanced at the clipboard on the receptionist's desk. "I haven't filled out the new patient paperwork yet."

Dr. Harper smiled. "No worries. You can bring it back with you and we'll go over it together."

Mallory nodded but stood in place, trying to calm the tremors that still coursed through her legs.

"I'm happy to stay, if you need me," Liam said quietly.

Mallory stared up at his face, studied his encouraging smile and wished she could borrow his strength if only for a moment.

"It's okay, Mallory," Dr. Harper said. "You're my only patient for today. If you're not ready to go back yet, that's fine. I can catch up on some paperwork and you can let me know when you'd like to start. Take all the time you'd like."

"No, thank you." Mallory picked up the new patient packet and walked toward the door. "I'm ready now." She glanced over her shoulder. "Thank you for your offer to stay, Liam, but I'll be fine. Please take Gayle for her latte." She smiled. "I wouldn't want her to have a reason to get upset with you."

Some of the concern in his eyes faded, a teasing light taking its place. "You're right. That wouldn't be good for any of us." He smiled gently. "We'll be back soon."

The exam room was small but comfortable and Dr. Harper took great care to help Mallory feel at ease. She spoke in soothing tones and asked questions in an unintimidating manner, waiting patiently as Mallory filled out the new patient packet, described her family's health history and spoke of her new job at Pine Creek Farm. Dr. Harper even managed to slip in a few jokes here and there, coaxing a laugh from Mallory when she least expected it.

"And when was your last checkup?" Dr. Harper asked.

Mallory, now lying on the exam table, stared up at the ceiling. Someone had taped a poster there. The scene was a serene landscape with a field of flowers. She traced each bloom with her eyes. "Last month."

"All was well, I take it?" Dr. Harper asked.

"Yes."

"Take a couple deep breaths for me, Mallory." Dr. Harper waited as Mallory did so, then said gently, "We'll take this slow, okay? At any time, if you feel uncomfortable or need a break, just let me know."

Mallory inhaled deeply again then released a long breath, feeling her heart rate slow slightly. "Okay."

Dr. Harper was gentle and quick and soon, the worst was over.

"All seems well now, too," Dr. Harper said, removing her gloves and pushing her stool back from the exam table. She stood and walked to Mallory's side. "Would you like to see your baby today? We received a grant last year that allowed us to purchase a new ultrasound machine. Our equipment's in-house and we can do a 3D ultrasound, if you'd like?"

Mallory closed her eyes briefly then refocused on the flowers. "Sure."

It didn't take long for Dr. Harper to set everything up and before long, a rhythmic heartbeat filled the room and the small monitor to the left of the exam table showed a baby's image.

"There he is," Dr. Harper said gently as she moved the transducer over the gel slicked across Mallory's belly. "A healthy baby boy."

Mallory, her mouth trembling, glanced at the screen once then stared at the flowers again. "Yes."

"Have you chosen a name?"

"No."

"Well, there's no rush. You still have several weeks before your due date. Lots of time to think about it."

Think. Mallory narrowed her eyes as she stared at the flowers. Thinking about her pregnancy was something she didn't want to do. Avoiding it as much as possible was less painful. But she no longer had that luxury, did she? Not if she wanted to give this baby—her son—the best life she possibly could.

Son. *My son*... How strange that sounded.

Mallory forced herself to look away from the flowers and face the monitor again. The baby's face was visible now—his small nose and parted lips clearly visible. His hand, delicate fingers curled, rested against his chin. He looked healthy and content. Peaceful.

"Could I..." She cleared her throat and blinked as a sheen of moisture gathered in her eyes. "May I have a picture of him, please?"

Dr. Harper smiled. "Of course. I'll email you this batch, but I think we can print at least one copy for you before you leave." She moved the transducer over Mallory's belly again, pressing a few buttons on the machine as she asked, "I'd like to ask you something a little more personal, if that's okay?"

Mallory nodded jerkily.

"How do you feel about the baby?"

A knot formed in Mallory's chest. It tightened then swelled, constricting her throat. "I—I don't know."

Dr. Harper remained silent.

"You know how this happened, right?" Mallory asked. "Jessie told them what I asked her to when she made the appointment, didn't she?"

"Yes. She filled us in on what she knew, but from this point forward, I'm here for you, Mallory. For whatever you'd like to tell me. And you don't have to share anything that you're not comfortable with."

"I'm keeping him," Mallory whispered.

When she didn't elaborate, Dr. Harper asked, "Have you met with a counselor, Mallory? Have you spoken to someone about what's happened to you?"

Mallory nodded. "It helped but..."

Dr. Harper waited a moment, then asked, "But what?"

Mallory didn't answer. She couldn't. The churn of her stomach and increasing pressure in her chest was overwhelming.

"You know," Dr. Harper said quietly. "For some of my

patients, they find comfort in journaling. Sometimes it helps to write your thoughts down. To get them on the outside. It can have a way of helping you reconcile your past with the future and help you find the strength to face it."

"I'm keeping him," Mallory repeated. "And I won't change my mind. I want to be a good mom, but sometimes..."

After a few moments, Dr. Harper covered Mallory's hand with her own and squeezed gently. "Write that thought down and try to finish it. See where it takes you. Then list the reasons you've decided to keep him. In time, you might find you're able to start a new list. One where you can explore the ways this baby might potentially bring you joy."

Mallory swallowed hard and repeated a soft refrain that seemed ingrained in her core. "I'll try."

Liam returned to the health clinic from the coffee shop and had been waiting with his mother in the waiting room for over an hour when Mallory finally emerged from the door beside the reception desk. Dr. Harper was with her, cupping her elbow and pointing at something Mallory held in her hands.

Liam glanced to his right where Gayle sat on a couch, a magazine open in her lap, her head rolling onto her left shoulder as she began to doze off. Apparently, the large caramel latte she'd ordered at the coffee shop had failed to fend off her late-morning fatigue.

"Mom?" He touched the back of her hand. "Mom? It's time to go."

Blinking, she sat up on the couch and looked around the room. A familiar expression of confusion appeared on her face as she studied her surroundings. She looked down at her lap and patted the magazine as though offering herself reassurance. "I'm reading."

Liam smiled. "I think you stopped reading some time ago. You got a good nap in while we waited." He stood and held out a hand for the magazine. "Mallory's all finished. It's time to go."

Gayle frowned, her eyes widening with fear. "Who's Mallory? Where am I?"

Liam sighed as a fresh wave of grief swept through him. He was used to this—the repeated questions and easily forgotten answers from his mother—but each time she asked something she'd already been told or had experienced firsthand, he was reminded of how rapidly her cognition had begun to decline. And being in a doctor's office, well, that was another painful reminder of the frequent medical appointments she'd had in the past and the many more that awaited her in the future. All of it was a reminder that his time with her was growing shorter.

"You know Mallory," he said quietly. "She's here to help us out. She read to you last night and helped you get settled in bed." He smiled. "She said you told her that you liked her voice better than mine."

Gayle frowned deeper, her brow furrowing as she tried to recall the information. He could see from the blank look in her eyes that the knowledge had failed to come to her.

"You're safe and sound, Mom. I promise." Liam reached down and removed the magazine from her lap then returned it to the table nearby. "Now, it's time to go."

He cupped her elbow and helped her to her feet, waiting for her to get her bearings for a moment before leading her across the waiting room to join Mallory.

"You're Liam, I'm guessing?" Dr. Harper looked at him, her brows raised.

"Yes," he said. "Liam Williams." He held out his hand. "It's nice to meet you. Thank you for helping Mallory today."

Dr. Harper smiled and shook his hand. "I was happy to. And I'm glad to meet you as well. I wanted to make sure Mallory had a ride home." She glanced at Mallory, who stood motionless, looking down at the item in her hands. "I'm afraid I wore her out with a ton of questions today—not to mention all the poking and prodding." She laughed. "I'm hoping I didn't scare her away from our next appointment."

Mallory looked up then and smiled, but her eyelids were pink and puffy as though she'd been crying. "Oh, no. I appreciate all you've done. Thank you, Dr. Harper."

"Remember to call me if you need anything," Dr. Harper said, before saying her goodbyes and returning to her office.

Liam led the way out of the clinic and into the parking lot, stepping back and holding the door at the exit, gesturing for Gayle and Mallory to precede him outside. "So, how'd it go?"

Mallory didn't answer. Instead, she continued taking slow steps behind Gayle, a small piece of paper still clutched tightly in her fist.

"Mallory, are you o—"

"Where am I?" Gayle, who'd walked ahead of them, stopped in the middle of the sidewalk and looked around urgently, a worried gleam in her eyes. "Where's my house? Where are the magnolias?"

Liam, hastening to reassure her, jogged a few steps to catch up with her and placed his palm on her back gently. "It's okay, Mom. We're in town. We came to the doctor's office where Mallory had an appointment and had a coffee while we waited." He pointed at his truck, which sat a few feet away in the parking lot. "There's my truck, see?"

"I want to go home," she said, her eyes wide and fearful as they met his. "I want to go home right now."

Liam hesitated and glanced over his shoulder. "Mallory said she needed to go by the bank on the way—"

But Mallory was no longer there.

He scanned the sidewalk and the surrounding area, glancing back at the front doors of the clinic, sweeping his gaze over the empty benches that were positioned outside the building and visually sifting through the people who strolled in front of the building. Finally, he noticed her standing near the bushes on one side of the building. Her back was to him, and she was doubled over, her shoulders heaving.

"Oh no," he whispered. "Mom, let's get you in the truck. I need to check on Mallory."

He ushered Gayle along the sidewalk and to the truck, helped her into the passenger seat then shut the door and jogged back to Mallory. By the time he reached her, she had straightened and stepped away from the bushes, one hand covering her mouth.

"Are you okay?" he asked.

She sure didn't look it. The color had drained from her face, leaving her cheeks pale, and despite the winter chill in the air, sweat had beaded on her forehead and along her temples beneath her hood.

"I—I'm okay." Her fingers, pressing a tissue to her lips, trembled as she spoke. "I just got sick all of a sudden. Too fast to make it back inside to the restroom." A bright red flush flooded her cheeks as she glanced up at him. "I'm so embarrassed."

"You shouldn't be," he said, issuing a wry smile. "I've heard it happens from time to time during a pregnancy." He dug around in the front pocket of his jeans then both of his back pockets before glancing over his shoulder at his truck. "I've got some clean napkins in the glove compartment of my truck. Give me just a second and I'll round you up a bottle of wa—"

"It's a boy."

He faced her again. Her fingers still touched her lips, muffling her words.

"I haven't told you that, have I?"

He shook his head.

"I've known it for over a month now, but I still haven't chosen a name." Tears welled onto her lower lashes. "I decided to keep him rather than give him up for adoption and I won't change my mind, but most days I don't want him. Most days, I don't even want to think about him." The tears broke free and poured unheeded down her red cheeks. Her eyes were full of anguish, so much so it broke his heart. "What kind of mother does that make me?"

Liam remained silent for moment. His fists clenched, a surge of anger rolling through him at the reminder of how she ended up in this position. He couldn't fathom how any man—especially one who professed to love a woman—could turn violent against her. It was no wonder she had difficulty trusting him.

The wounded vulnerability in her gaze prompted his fists to unfurl. His arms ached to wrap protectively around her, hug her close and tuck her head beneath his chin.

Instead, he stepped closer, reached out and eased the small piece of paper from her free hand. It was an ultrasound picture, the baby's face clearly visible. He blew out a heavy breath as he imagined her in Dr. Harper's office, facing the image of her future child—and the weight of her past—alone.

"Considering all you've been through?" he said. "I'd say it makes you human."

A small sob escaped her. She looked up at him, some of the pain receding from her eyes, then she shoved the tissue she held into the pocket of her coat, wiped the tears from her cheeks and nodded.

It was a long, quiet drive back to the farm. Gayle, exhausted from the morning's events, had fallen asleep in the passenger seat, her head leaning against the headrest. Mallory, seated in the back of the cab, stared silently out the window, lost deep in thought. Neither of them had been eager to visit the bank after leaving the doctor's office, so he headed straight home.

After arriving at the farm, Liam assisted Gayle and Mallory out of the truck then led Gayle upstairs and helped her into bed, removing her shoes and socks and covering her with a warm quilt before shutting the door quietly behind him as he left. He found Mallory in the empty guest room across from her bedroom. She stood in the center of the room, her hands twisting together below her protruding belly as she gazed about the room.

"I don't know what I'm doing," she whispered.

Liam entered the room and stood beside her. "Not many of us do."

"I mean, I don't even know where to begin," she said.

He smiled. "You could start with the walls."

She glanced up at him, her blue eyes wide with surprise. "The walls?"

"I know blue is the usual color people pick for a boy's nursery," he said softly. "But there's no rule about it. We can paint the walls whatever color you like. Yellow might be a good choice for a boy. Or we could paint them green, leave them white or go with patterned wallpaper even. The choice is yours."

She returned her attention to the room, her eyes roving slowly over the walls, the floor and the empty corners.

"We'll need a crib," he continued. "And a bassinet, for when you want to keep him in your room. We'll need a changing table, rocking chair, or a glider, maybe. A glider might be more comfortable."

She nodded slowly.

"We can start there," he repeated. "I can give Pam a call. Ask her and the ladies' group to come by tomorrow and help you decide on the details. It'd give you a chance to meet everyone. Have a support network when you need it. Do you think you'd be up for that?"

Her chest lifted on a deep inhale as she glanced around the room again. "Yes," she said. "I think I'm up for that."

"Good. I'll go grab you some paper and a pen and I'll bring a snack with it in case you get hungry. Mom's napping, so you can take your time. Brainstorm some ideas of things you might like. Write it down."

Her gaze strayed to the window as she whispered, "Yes. I'll write it down."

Nodding, Liam left and walked downstairs. He found a pen and notepad, washed and sliced an apple, and poured milk into a glass. It wasn't until he'd loaded it all onto a tray and began walking back upstairs that he realized he was humming a lullaby.

And he realized that when he'd made suggestions to Mallory for preparing for the baby, he hadn't said *you*. He'd said *we*.

That night, after Mallory helped Gayle into bed and read from the Bible until she fell asleep, Mallory went back to her own room, grabbed the notepad and pen Liam had provided earlier in the day and sat on the edge of the bed. It was dark out, but the stars were shining outside the window and Liam was probably admiring them right now in his chair by the firepit behind the house where he'd gone to relax after dinner.

The house was quiet and still. It was, Mallory supposed, the best time to begin.

She uncapped the pen and scanned the words she'd written on the first page hours earlier in the guest room across the hall.

Crib, bassinet, changing table, diapers, onesies, baby wipes—

She stopped reading and looked up, her eyes peering out the window into the dark fields beyond. Inhaling deeply, she turned the page to a blank sheet and began writing.

*I want to be a good mom, but sometimes—*she paused, squeezed the pen tightly in her hand, then continued writing—*I don't want him.*

A shaky breath escaped her. She lifted her head and stared out the window again for a few moments then returned her attention to the page in front of her and wrote again.

On the days that I do want him, I think of how he's not to blame for his father's sins. How innocent and how precious he is. This new life that's growing inside me.

On the days I want him, I remind myself that he's a part of me as well. But I wonder if he'll be like me. I wonder if he'll look like me or if he'll look more like Tr—

Her hand froze around the pen. Heart pounding, she left the sentence unfinished, dropped down to the next blank line on the page, and wrote again.

What color would you like the walls... Oliver?

"Oliver," she whispered. A small smile curved her lips.

Do you like that name? It was my father's name. Sometimes people called him Ollie, but only those who knew him very well.

What do you think, Oliver? Would you like me to paint the walls of your nursery blue? Yellow? Or maybe you'd prefer something more rustic, like green. A forest green, maybe? The same green that I'm sure will fill the fields here on Liam's farm when spring arrives—the same time you're supposed to be here.

You'd like Liam, I think. He's patient. Kind. Gentle. Understanding.

The words blurred and she blinked hard.

Who will you be like, Oliver? Who will you be?

Chapter Six

The next afternoon, Mallory took her first step toward trying to be a good mother.

Liam helped her prepare. Earlier that morning, after he, Mallory and Gayle had eaten breakfast, he'd rounded up several chairs and a folding table, carried them upstairs to the empty guest room and positioned the chairs around the table in a comfortable circle.

"For the ladies' group," he said, smiling.

True to his promise, Liam had called Pam Marshall, leader of the ladies' group at his church, the day prior and invited her and the other women to Pine Creek Farm to meet Mallory and help her brainstorm ideas for the nursery. Liam had left soon after setting up the table and chairs and had gone to work, feeding the horses and helping the hands muck the stalls while Mallory stayed indoors with Gayle. Anxious for the afternoon meeting, Mallory had busied herself with reading to Gayle and doing chores about the house while Gayle watched late morning talk shows.

By lunchtime, the ladies' group arrived with three large baskets. One basket had been filled to the brim with warm barbecue sandwiches, which they carried to the stable and distributed to Liam and the hands. The second basket, the largest of the three, held lunch for the ladies, which consisted of barbecued chicken, seasoned turnips, potato salad and warm peach cobbler for dessert. And after all the ladies finished eating, Pam Marshall gave Mallory the third basket and smiled.

"It's from all of us." Seated in one of the chairs Liam had carried into the guest room, Pam glanced around her at the other ladies, who sat around the table, then looked at Mallory. "It's only a start, mind you. We'd like to hold a proper baby shower for you closer to your due date, if you wouldn't mind?"

Wendy Owens, seated to Pam's left, scooted forward in her chair. "Oh, yes, please. We haven't had a proper baby shower in ages." She nudged her glasses higher on her nose. "All those cute decorations and baby clothes..." She sighed. "It'd be a dream day!"

Barbara Smith and Cherie Ann Little, who sat on either side of Gayle, nodded in agreement. "A dream day," they repeated in unison, then looked at each other and burst out laughing.

Mallory smiled. Liam had been right. She enjoyed spending time with the ladies' group. Pam Marshall had a cheerful disposition and spoke with a relaxed confidence and the rest of the older women were kind, easygoing and laughed often. Mallory liked them immediately.

"So," Pam said, "have you decided what color you'd like to paint the nursery walls yet?"

"There's no rush," Barbara said.

"Not at all." Cherie Ann motioned toward the big basket sitting on the table in front of Mallory. "Maybe you should open your gift first and then decide."

Mallory shifted in her seat to a more comfortable position then pulled the basket closer to her. "Thank you so much for this. I hope you know I didn't expect you to bring anything today or go to all this trouble."

"Oh, it was no trouble," Pam said. "We were thrilled when Liam called and invited us over. We always like to welcome our neighbors to Pine Creek." She glanced at Mallory's belly and smiled. "Even the smallest ones who have yet to arrive."

Mallory's smile quivered but she managed to hold it in place as she untied the bow on the white basket, peeled away the plastic covering and began removing items.

There were bibs of every color and design, several blue-and-white onesies, a pacifier, teething ring and plush blue teddy bear.

"There are so many beautiful things here." Mallory lined the items up on the table, tears springing to her eyes. "How did you manage this on such short notice?"

Wendy grinned. "When Liam called yesterday, we met up and took a trip into town."

"Liam told us you're having a boy. That's why we got a lot of blue onesies." Cherie Ann bit her lip and leaned forward, propping her elbows on the table. "I hope he was right."

"Of course he was right," Barbara said. "Liam's always right." She glanced at Gayle, who sat beside her. "Isn't that right, Gayle? I can't remember a time when Liam was wrong about anything. You raised him to be a fine man. So honorable and kind. I don't think I've met another man quite like him."

Gayle looked at Barbara blankly.

"He stayed, you know," Barbara continued, looking at Mallory. "Years ago, when Liam's father left the farm, Holt followed his dad back to the rodeo circuit, but Liam stayed here. He loved his mother too much to leave her to handle the farm on her own. Even at eighteen, he was already mature far beyond his years."

Mallory looked down and fiddled with the white ribbon tied around the plush teddy bear. "Did Liam ever leave Pine Creek Farm? I mean, for college or to explore another career?"

Barbara shook her head. "But he could have, certainly."

"Liam is one of the smartest men I've ever met," Pam said. "He could've gone to school anywhere and pursued any profession he wanted, but he chose to stay here and support his mother."

"And he never…" Mallory hesitated, winding the silky ribbon around her index finger then unwinding it. "Has he ever been married?"

"No," Pam said softly. When Mallory glanced up and met her eyes, she smiled. "Gayle shared with us once, years ago, that she'd tried to encourage him to branch out and live for himself a bit more. To maybe even leave Pine Creek for a while and devote his energy to his own pursuits. But he declined. She confided that she'd asked him once if he resented his decision to stay over the years or if he regretted the opportunities he'd missed out on." She glanced at Gayle with a tender expression. "She said he told her no. That staying with her and running the farm had been the right thing to do."

Mallory fell silent, turning the phrase over in her mind, rubbing the silky ribbon between her fingertips.

Because it's the right thing to do.

For some reason, the words settled in her belly like a heavy stone. They drew her shoulders down and made her sag against the edge of the table.

"I like the bear," Gayle said. "That shade of blue." Her hazel eyes fixed on the stuffed toy in front of Mallory and the crow's-feet beside her eyes wrinkled as she smiled. "I gave my son, Holt, one like it. He loved it so."

Her smile returning, Mallory picked it up and passed the teddy bear across the table to Gayle. "Here. Hold it. It's even softer than it looks."

Gayle held the teddy bear that Mallory passed her, cradling it in her hands gently and smoothing her thumbs over its furry ears. "It's such a beautiful shade of blue."

"Liam said we could choose any color for the walls," Mallory said. "But I do like the idea of blue for a boy." She looked at Gayle's hands, watching the older woman's ivory fingers gently smooth down the teddy bear's fur. "Gayle, I think if you and I take the bear to a paint store, they may be able to match that shade and create a custom paint for the nursery."

Gayle looked up from the teddy bear and glanced around the room. She stared at the white walls, her brow furrowing as she considered Mallory's idea. "Yes." She smiled brightly and patted the teddy bear. "This blue. The exact same shade."

"Well, there you go," Pam said. "That's one decision made already." She looked at Mallory. "Do you have a piece of paper that we can use to start writing these decisions down?"

Mallory nodded and picked up the notepad Liam had given her. She opened it, flipped to a blank page, grabbed a pen and smiled at the other women. "So which decision should we tackle next?"

They brainstormed for over an hour, discussing each item on the list of needs Mallory had made for the nursery, batting around ideas for different themes, discussing various patterns in terms of blankets and rugs, then chatted about postpartum recovery, 3:00 a.m. feedings and the many other challenges that naturally arose from having a baby in the house.

At one point, Pam pointed out how Liam could be of help by suggesting that Mallory ask him to childproof the electrical outlets and cabinets and, on occasion, change diapers, which made Cherie Ann cackle out loud. Laughter was had by all, and Mallory found herself giggling on more than one occasion, something she hadn't done naturally in what seemed like forever.

The women reminded her of her mother, whom she lost years ago, and sitting at the table, surrounded by strong, patient women who spoke with joy at the prospect of a new baby gave Mallory hope.

Hope that she might be able to be a good mother after all.

When they arrived at the last item on the list, Mallory jotted down ideas each of the ladies shared then rubbed the small of her back. A small ache had begun a half hour ago but she'd enjoyed the camaraderie with the women so much, she hadn't wanted to interrupt their conversations by leaving the table.

"Oh, Mallory," Pam said, pushing back from the table. "Here we are babbling away with you sitting in one position all this time. I imagine your back must be hurting by now."

Mallory smiled and waved away the concern. "I'm okay."

She was used to pain. The twinge in her back was simply a minor inconvenience.

The thought of her past, however brief, tugged her mouth back into a frown and she pushed her chair back from the table as well then stood. "I just need to stretch my legs, is all."

Rubbing the small of her back with one hand, she strolled across the room toward the window. It was late afternoon now, and outside, Liam led several horses and riders in a line across the front field of Pine Creek Farm, heading back to the stable.

"Liam and the hands took the horses out," Mallory said.

"Liam takes great care of those horses," Pam said. "It's chilly out there but no matter the weather, he makes sure they get their exercise and fresh air."

"And how his business has grown," Wendy said. "He told Pam yesterday on the phone that the guesthouses are almost completely booked for spring already. You must be so proud of his success, Gayle."

Mallory glanced over her shoulder and noticed Gayle gazed back at Wendy without recognition.

"She is," Cherie Ann said before addressing Gayle. "You've told us so many times over the years about how much you love him."

Gayle looked down at the teddy bear in her hands. "I love babies," she said quietly.

Cherie Ann leaned forward and patted Gayle's knee. "Looks like you'll have one around the farm soon enough. From what Liam told us, Mallory's baby boy will be here in March. That's only a couple months away."

Gayle looked up again and turned her head to focus on Mallory. Her gaze drifted down to Mallory's protruding belly as though seeing it for the first time.

"Oh, a baby." Smiling, Gayle stood and walked across the room to join Mallory at the window. She reached out and placed her warm palms on Mallory's belly. "I've always wanted a grandbaby."

For a moment, Mallory stiffened. Gayle's hands, though gentle, cradled the large swell of Mallory's expectant belly, a gesture that brought the reality of the baby into stark relief. Gayle's touch, the kind Mallory had avoided herself over the past seven months, was a tactile sensation that Mallory couldn't ignore.

Pam stood, her gaze concerned, as she studied Mallory's expression. "Gayle, Mallory's back is bothering her. It might not be comfortable for her to have others—"

"It's okay," Mallory whispered, somehow managing to smile, lift her arms and cover Gayle's hands with her own. "There's definitely a baby in here, isn't there?"

Gayle met her eyes, a look of longing on her face that made Mallory want to hug her.

"It's a boy," Mallory said.

Gayle smiled wider. "I had a baby boy once. May I hold him when he gets here?"

Mallory nodded.

Gayle glanced at the women behind them, who watched them both with soft smiles and teary eyes. "I'll be able to hold the baby." Then she faced the window again and looked out as the men rode the horses across the grounds. She pointed at Liam. "That man there. Leading them all. He's here a lot." She glanced at Mallory expectantly. "Is he your husband? The baby's father?"

A heavy sensation settled within Mallory again. She slipped away from Gayle's touch and lowered her hands back to her side. "No," she whispered. "No, he's not."

The winter wind blew cold across the grounds of Pine Creek Farm but Liam, having led the horses on a trail ride, was warm enough inside the stable to shed his jacket. He did so, setting it aside, then resumed brushing his favorite mare, Sugar.

"It's only been a few days," he said, "but I think it's going to work out."

"Sounds like it." Jessie's voice, strong and clear, emitted from the speaker of his cell phone from where it sat on the ledge of a nearby stall. "I told Holt I might drive down there this weekend and check on how things were going, but it seems like everything's well in hand."

"So far." Liam bent and brushed the underside of Sugar's belly. "The visit to the doctor yesterday was a bit rougher than Mallory expected but she pulled through it just fine."

"I was afraid that'd be difficult for her," Jessie said. "How did she react when she came out?"

Liam winced as he recalled the pallor of Mallory's face when she'd emerged from her checkup with the doctor yesterday. She'd been nervous, frightened and embarrassed by the way her body had responded to the stress she'd endured. "She did as well as one could expect."

"Has she spoken with you about the baby?"

"A little." Liam straightened and smiled as Sugar nudged him with her nose. "She's gradually getting used to the idea, I think. After the doctor's visit yesterday, we spoke a little bit about putting the nursery together. I called Pam Marshall this morning and asked her if she and the ladies' group would stop by and visit Mallory. Help her come up with some ideas for decorating the nursery and all."

"That was a wonderful idea," Jessie said, her tone brightening. "Did they come? And did Mallory get along well with them?"

"They seemed to hit it off. I didn't stick around the house long. I introduced them, helped Pam carry some barbecue sandwiches to the guys down here at the stable then went back to work." He rubbed Sugar behind her ears. "They're still up at the house now, I think, brainstorming plans for the nursery."

Or at least he thought so. When he and the hands had

returned with the horses at the end of the trail ride, the ladies' cars had still been parked in the driveway.

"Good," Jessie said. "Decorating the nursery might help take her mind off her worries for a while. It might give her something positive to focus on."

Liam smiled. "She's having a boy. Had she told you that?"

Jessie laughed. "No, but what better place for a little boy to be introduced to the world than Pine Creek Farm?"

"A little boy would love it here." Liam grinned, thinking of all the fun and—sometimes—trouble he and Holt had gotten into as kids when rollicking around the farm. "By spring, there'll be grass as far as the eye can see in the fields. We can throw a blanket out and he can roll around on it beneath the sun to his heart's content. We'll show him the animals—I think he'd like the horses. Most kids do. And it'll be warmer then. We can rock him to sleep on the porch at night while the stars are shining. There's no better lullaby in the world than the crickets and frogs singing down by the pond at night."

He laughed, recalling the many times he and Holt had traipsed around the pond on a back lot behind the house. They'd spent most of each summer digging for crawdads in the mud, skipping stones across the water and catching bream.

"When he gets older," Liam said, "I'll take him out there and show him how to fish. The pond's probably stocked to the brim by now since I haven't fished in it lately. The little guy'll probably catch something as soon as he drops his cork in the water."

Smiling at the thought of teaching a little boy how to fish like he and Holt used to, Liam patted Sugar's back. It took a moment for him to realize that Jessie had grown silent on the other end of the line.

"Jessie? You still there?"

"Yeah," she said softly. "I'm just wondering how long you plan on Mallory and her son staying at Pine Creek Farm? The things you're speaking of, Mallory's son wouldn't be able to do for years. And Gayle, well…"

She didn't have to finish the sentence out loud. He already knew.

"Taking the job at Pine Creek Farm is supposed to be a new beginning for Mallory," Jessie said. "It was never intended to be an end."

Liam stilled. "I know."

As though sensing his tension, Sugar nudged his chest with her nose again.

"Do you?" Jessie asked. "Maybe it's not Mallory's baby you're thinking of. Maybe it's a son of your own," she said gently. "Having Mallory and a new baby at Pine Creek Farm may have just reminded you of what you want in life. It might have made you think of all the things you may have had to put off over the years to take care of Gayle."

Was that it? Was that what had prompted the thoughts of a boy growing up on the farm? Was the thought of Mallory's baby boy simply a reminder of the family he had once wished he'd have one day? A prospect that seemed less and less achievable as each year had passed.

He tried to envision it. Tried to picture a child—a little boy—who wasn't Mallory's son, but his own. A child who might one day belong to him and his wife.

In the past, he'd been afraid to allow himself to dwell on such wishes. He'd kept his focus on Gayle instead. And now it was difficult to imagine it. To see, in his mind's eye, a woman who wasn't Mallory living at the farm and raising a child—who wasn't Mallory's—with him.

The discomfort that moved through him at the thought of Mallory and her child leaving shocked him.

"I'm just excited at the thought of having a kid around," Liam said, trying to reassure himself as much as Jessie. "I just got carried away, I guess."

"It's easy to do," Jessie said gently. "I just want you to be aware of that. It's so much easier than you know to get attached to the children who you help."

And it'd be easy to get attached to Mallory, as well.

She didn't need to say that out loud either. He got the message—loud and clear.

Liam cleared his throat and patted Sugar's back. "Of course. I was just thinking out loud for a minute. Just random thoughts. Nothing necessarily tied to Mallory and her baby."

And the excitement he'd felt at decorating the nursery, that was just another byproduct of the idea of having a family. An idea he'd indulged in years ago but had packed away in the darkest recesses of his heart to focus on running the farm. Mallory's arrival had just prompted its reemergence. That was all.

He'd just have to be careful from this point forward and keep an eye out for getting too attached to Mallory and her baby.

"You're doing a great thing, Liam," Jessie said. "Helping Mallory get back on her feet and make a fresh start for herself and her baby is a wonderful thing to do. It'll change their lives for the better and they'll always remember you for it."

It was a pleasant sentiment. One he should welcome. But for some reason, the thought of Mallory and her baby moving on, leaving Pine Creek Farm—and him—behind sent a fresh wave of disappointment through him.

"In the meantime, I'm only a call away," Jessie said. "If you ever need me to come down to help with Mallory or the baby, or if you or Mallory have any questions, just give me a call. Otherwise, I'm going to give Mallory space and time to settle in before the baby comes."

Liam put the brush down, led Sugar into her stall then picked up the phone. "Thank you, Jessie. If we need you, I won't hesitate to contact you."

They said their goodbyes and Liam disconnected the call. He shoved the cell phone in the back pocket of his jeans then stood in front of Sugar's stall, rubbing the mare's forehead and allowing his mind to drift, just for moment, back to the happy images of him fishing with a little boy. A son he could help support and raise. A son he could guide through life, instilling strong values within him and show-ing him the ropes at the farm. A son who would grow up into a strong man and carry a little piece of Liam—hope-fully, the best part—throughout his life, and pass on the lessons to a new generation.

It was a sweet dream. As sweet as it had always been. But, like most of the dreams he'd had in his thirty-eight years of life, it would likely never come to fruition.

"Liam?"

He started as Mallory's voice and soft footsteps echoed around the quiet stable. The hands, having brushed their horses and settled them in their stalls for the day, had left over half an hour ago to check the grounds and carry on with chores.

"I'm back here," he called out.

She walked into view then, rounding the line of stalls and strolling toward him. She was bundled up in her warm coat again, her hood firmly in place, as always, and she turned her head from one side to the other, smiling at each horse as she passed them.

"We saw you and the hands riding the horses earlier," she said. "Did you get cold on your ride?"

He patted Sugar's back then stepped away from the stall. "No. We've gotten used to the chilly temps and the horses enjoy getting out several times a week for some exercise." He leaned to the side, glancing at the entrance of the stable. "Did you bring Pam and the ladies with you?"

Mallory shook her head. "They left a little while ago. Gayle was getting tired so I helped her get settled in bed and then Pam and the ladies helped me clean up. They left not long after and told me to give you their regards."

Liam smiled. "I wish they'd have stopped by the stable before they left. The crew couldn't stop talking about how good those barbecue sandwiches were and ate so many they were like slugs afterward. I almost had to lay down the law to get them back up on their feet and working again."

Mallory smiled back. "They stuffed me and your mom to the gills, too. They brought quite a spread—and gifts for the baby. They're wonderful women. Thank you for introducing me to them."

Nodding, Liam shoved his hands in his pockets. "You're welcome. It's good for you to have some friends other than me in Pine Creek. That way you'll have plenty of people to lean on when you need help."

She stared back at him, blushing. "Friends?"

"Yeah."

"You've been a great friend to me already," she said quietly. "And to the baby." Her hands lifted slowly and covered her round belly, cradling it gently. "You've been the best friend I've had in a very long time."

Maybe it was the tenderness in her eyes as she looked at him or the gratitude in her smile. Or maybe it was the way her graceful hands cradled the baby she carried, her cheeks flushed and her touch gentle. Whatever it was, in that moment, she was the most beautiful woman he'd ever laid eyes on.

"I, uh…" He looked down at his boots. Tapped his right toe twice. "Would you like to meet Sugar now?"

"Yes, please."

She walked over and stood beside him at the stall, the sweet scent of her shampoo drifting in, surrounding him.

He cleared his throat. "I think I told you the day we arrived that Sugar's ten years old."

Mallory nodded.

"You been around horses much?" he asked.

"Not at all." She studied Sugar, a slow smile curving her lips. "But I'm not afraid of them."

"That's good," he said. "Sugar's gentle. Would you like to pet her?"

"Yes, please."

"Put your hand out, near her nose," he said. "Give her a chance to catch your scent and get to know you a little bit."

She hesitated, glancing at him then the mare, then lifted her right hand and held it near Sugar's nose. The mare leaned forward, her nostrils flared, sniffed Mallory's palm and then, seemingly satisfied with the introduction, nudged her fingers with her soft nose.

"Oh!" Mallory stroked Sugar's forehead and neck, laughing as the mare edged forward and pressed closer. "She's very friendly."

"Yep." Liam smirked. "The exact opposite of that cat that hangs around here. Which reminds me…" He walked over to a metal bucket that sat by the wall. "It's close to feeding time. Might as well put the food out now for when Miss Priss ambles in later."

"Liam?"

He removed the lid, grabbed a scooper and scooped up a hefty amount of dry food. "Yeah?"

"I think Miss Priss is already here."

Liam poured the dry cat food into a metal bowl and put it on the floor. "Doubt it. She would've attacked me by now."

"Maybe not."

He replaced the lid on the bucket, turned around and froze. "Well, would you look at that?"

There she was, Miss Priss, winding affectionately around Mallory's legs.

"I'm not scared of Sugar," Mallory whispered, "but this cat's another story altogether. Is it okay for me to move?"

Liam held up his hand. "No. Stay still. I don't want her jumping on you like she does me."

They stood, frozen in place, as Miss Priss continued winding around Mallory's legs. After a couple minutes, Miss Priss walked lazily over to the bowl Liam had put on the floor and, after eyeing him warily, began eating.

"Well, would you look at that?" Liam repeated.

"Oh!" Mallory jumped, her hands pressing against her belly.

Liam sprang toward her, glancing over his shoulder to make sure the cat was still eating several feet away. Miss Priss, obviously hungry, stayed put and ate despite the distraction.

He sighed with relief then looked at Mallory. "What is it? Are you okay?"

She smiled wide, her eyes bright with excitement. It was an expression he hadn't seen her make before. "Yeah."

Laughter escaped her. "Oliver just kicked. I was so focused on the cat that it caught me off guard."

Liam smiled. "Oliver? You decided on a name?"

"Yes."

"It's a fine name." Caught up in the moment, he lifted his hand and stepped towards her then stopped. "If you don't mind my asking, what does it feel like when he kicks? Does it hurt?"

"No," she said, smiling down at her belly. "At least, not this time. It was like a strong nudge against my belly button."

Liam grinned. "Maybe Oliver liked having Miss Priss visit you."

She laughed and he caught his breath, savoring the cheerful sound. "Maybe so, because there he goes again."

Her eyes met his and her hand lifted, too. An expectant look crossed her face as her mouth parted. For a moment, he thought she might ask what he was silently hoping for. He thought she might reach out, take his hand in hers and place it on her belly to feel the baby's movement. To share in the moment.

But she didn't.

Instead, her cheeks flushed and she stepped back, lowering her hand to her side. "I think I've interrupted you enough." She motioned toward the cat. "I'll get out of your hair now and let you get back to what you were doing."

With that, she spun on her heel and walked away. He watched her leave then returned to Sugar's stall and stroked the mare's back, allowing himself to imagine—just once more—what it might be like to have a son.

That night, before going to sleep, Mallory opened her notepad and wrote to Oliver again.

I haven't told you about Sugar yet, have I? She's a brown

mare—ten years old—and she's Liam's favorite horse. I was able to pet her today.

She smiled at the memory.

Her nose was soft and warm, and her whiskers tickled my palm when she sniffed my hand. She's so friendly and gentle. She leans against you when you pet her and when you stop, she nudges your hand with her nose to continue. Maybe one day when it's warm, after you've arrived, I might ask Liam to show me how to ride her.

She stopped writing and tapped the pen against her lips before continuing.

Maybe, if we're still at Pine Creek Farm when you're old enough, he'll teach you how to ride, too.

She stopped writing and glanced over her shoulder at the closed door. Gayle had gone to bed long ago and was sleeping soundly in her room. Liam was sitting outside by the firepit again, gazing at the stars.

Mallory began writing again.

I hope you like Liam and Gayle as much as I do. It was Liam's idea to start putting together your nursery and I think he's excited to see it all come together. A few ladies from his church visited me today and we made plans for decorations that I hope you'll like.

Gayle is Liam's mother. She's forgotten quite a lot of her past due to her illness, but one thing she remembers well is that she's always wanted a grandbaby, and even though you're not hers, she's anxious to hold you.

Mallory smiled.

I think that would make her happy. You, Oliver, will make her happy.

Mallory stopped writing. "Do you know what would make me happy?" she whispered out loud. "Do you know what I wish for you?"

She put the pen down and closed her eyes, silently answering the question with words she didn't have the courage to speak or write.

I wish you had a dad like Liam.

Chapter Seven

Chilly winter wind blew across the grounds of Pine Creek Farm for the remainder of January and throughout February. But soon the air warmed, the days grew longer and the sun shined bright. By the second week of March, the dormant grass in the fields had turned green and sprang to life. Tiny yellow wildflowers dotted the landscape and lush, healthy leaves filled every branch of the trees. But the most magnificent sight was the bounty of full blooms gracing the magnolia trees that lined the driveway leading to the main house.

"It's beautiful," Mallory said.

And it was—even more than she'd imagined two months ago when standing in the same spot on the day she'd arrived at Pine Creek Farm.

She tipped her head back for a better view of the flowery branches that towered overhead as she stood at the edge of the paved driveway. Against the backdrop of the clear blue sky, the fragrant blooms, high above, resembled thick downy feathers that danced and fluttered in the warm spring breeze.

"I told you that you would love it," Gayle said as she stood beside her.

Mallory glanced at Gayle and smiled. She and Gayle had

grown close over the past two months, eating every meal together, taking long walks along the property in the afternoon and reading from the Bible each night. Though Gayle's memory had continued to deteriorate, she had grown accustomed to Mallory and though she couldn't recall Mallory's name on some days, she seemed to still recognize her face and welcome her presence on the majority of occasions.

The more comfortable Gayle grew in her presence, the more accomplished Mallory had begun to feel as a caretaker. When she'd first arrived at Pine Creek Farm, she'd been eager to earn her own way and contribute to the farm. Ensuring Gayle was well cared for and comfortable had helped her feel as though she had done just that and when the spring guests had begun to arrive two weeks ago, populating the guest houses and two of the rooms on the first floor of the main house, she was able to help even more. Every morning, she set her alarm and woke up early, joined Liam downstairs and helped cook breakfast for the guests.

Mallory pulled her attention away from the magnolia trees and gazed across the front field of Pine Creek Farm where Liam, sitting astride Sugar, led a trail ride for guests. She smiled. Mornings had become her favorite part of the day. It wasn't just the bright sun, the warm spring air and cheerful chirp of birds. It was being greeted by Liam's smile when she descended the stairs and joined him in the kitchen. It was the easy conversation and familiar rhythm they fell into every day as they cooked breakfast together that made her smile each night when she went to bed and look forward to getting up the next morning.

But despite the increasing joy she'd discovered at the farm and the recent change in season, not every day had been easy.

Mallory rubbed the small of her back where a constant

ache had taken up residence two weeks ago. Oliver had grown. Each day that passed reminded her that her due date was approaching faster than ever. If the increasing ache in her legs and back, ever-growing belly and sometimes-overwhelming fatigue didn't remind her, the calendar did.

Nine days. That was it. Nine days were all that separated her from being a mother.

"What are we going to do now?"

Mallory blinked and refocused on Gayle, who looked at her with raised brows. Though Gayle had grown comfortable in Mallory's presence, she still remained on edge about each day's events. Being at home in familiar surroundings offered Gayle a tremendous sense of security, but her disorientation regarding the present day and time led her to seek frequent reassurance for what lay before her each day.

Every morning, as they ate breakfast together, Mallory would detail the itinerary of the day to Gayle and remind her throughout the afternoon of the plans she had for them, which usually included an outdoor activity since the warmer weather had arrived and the grounds were so beautiful. Sunshine, fresh air and being surrounded by the cheerful chatter of guests who strolled along the grounds always seemed to lift Gayle's spirits.

Mallory grinned. "We're going to dig in the dirt, remember? We've got several batches of Wave petunias by the front porch and we're going to start planting them today."

That was, if her body held out long enough. A sharp twinge moved through the small of her back and she rubbed the spot a bit harder.

She'd grown accustomed to the aches and pains of pregnancy over the past two months but lately—the past few days, especially—they seemed more frequent and intense. With her due date fast approaching, she'd tried to prepare as best as she could and rest whenever possible. She'd begun taking naps in the afternoon, returning to her bedroom after settling Gayle down for her daily rest, crawling into her own bed and getting as much extra sleep as she could until Gayle woke again. Lying down with her feet propped up on a pillow had become a luxury—her favorite indulgence—and she found herself looking forward to it today as well.

"It's around eleven o'clock," Mallory told Gayle. That was something else she'd learned about Gayle: knowing the time put Gayle's mind at ease so she reminded her of it often. "We'll plant petunias for an hour then go in and have lunch. After that, you'll probably be ready for your nap."

Gayle pondered this information. She narrowed her eyes and looked up at the magnolia trees again then glanced across the grounds at Liam, who led guests on a horseback ride across the field. After a moment, she nodded in agreement, spun on her heel and began walking toward the main house.

"Well, come on then," Gayle called over her shoulder as she walked. "Those petunias aren't gonna plant themselves, are they?"

Laughing, Mallory followed.

Thirty minutes later, she and Gayle had settled comfortably on the soft grass by the flower beds in front of the main house. They'd planted several petunia plants in a row and were patting the last plant into the ground before moving on to the second row.

"Getting tired yet?" Mallory asked, glancing at Gayle.

Gayle shook her head and the wide-brimmed straw hat Mallory had insisted she wear flopped over her forehead. "Got more to do," she said. "There's a whole nother row to plant."

"Yes, but if you get tired, we can always go in." And

considering the achy fatigue that had taken up residence in Mallory's back, she'd welcome the rest.

"I'm fine." Gayle's eyes were heavy, but she smiled as she looked down and patted Mallory's belly. "How's the baby today?"

Mallory shifted to a more comfortable position on the ground and shrugged. "He seems content. But he's kicking quite a bit."

Gayle grinned. "He's ready to get out of there."

One of the horses walking across the grounds behind them neighed. The relaxed and somewhat playful sound echoed across the field and caught Gayle's attention.

"Such beautiful horses," she breathed.

Mallory glanced over her shoulder, smiling as Liam waved in their direction. "Yes." She waved back. "They are beautiful."

As was Liam.

Heat engulfed her face and she quickly lowered her arm to her side then returned her attention to the plant in front of her. She resumed patting damp soil around the base of the petunia, trying to keep her thoughts from straying back to Liam.

She wasn't sure when her feelings for Liam had grown but at some point over the past two months, she'd begun to take notice of and admire the many admirable traits that he possessed.

One, he smiled every morning. She knew there were mornings when he was exhausted, overworked and probably aching from the amount of physical labor he had to undertake on the farm. But no matter his physical state or mood, he never failed to greet her with a cheery disposition and optimistic outlook for the day.

Loving his mother was another great quality he possessed. No matter how busy his day might be, Liam always made time for Gayle, returning to the main house for lunch every day, answering questions repeatedly with patience and understanding on the days Gayle had trouble remembering the answers. And, most notably of all, he never failed to visit her room every night when she settled in bed to kiss her forehead and whisper that he loved her.

His hands, though big and strong, were gentle as he brushed his horses and stroked their backs, murmuring sweet phrases of praise. He'd even managed to come to some type of understanding with Miss Priss. Two months ago, after Miss Priss had introduced herself to Mallory, the cat had taken up following Mallory and Gayle around the grounds whenever they emerged outside. And the cat would follow Mallory, without fail, into the stable every evening when she would join Liam by Sugar's stall to visit with the mare. On each occasion, she'd noticed Liam smile at the sight of the cat winding around Mallory's legs and rubbing her cheek against Mallory's shoes.

"It must be Oliver," he had said once, grinning. "Miss Priss knows you're expecting."

She could still recall his expression, the gentle indulgence in his eyes as he'd gazed adoringly at her belly. It had stolen her breath the first time he'd looked at her in that way.

That may have been it. That may have been the moment that she'd begun to think of Liam differently than a friend. That look may have been what prompted her to wonder silently—but keeping her thoughts a careful secret—how it might feel to be loved by Liam. To be cared for by him in the same way that he cared for his mother. To have a kind, honorable man like him protect and support her every day and do the same for Oliver.

It was all these wonderful traits and more that had prompted her to imagine what her life might've been like if she'd met Liam before Trevor.

A slight sense of dismay unfurled deep in her belly at the reminder of her past…but at least it didn't weigh so heavily on her now as it had before. Pam Marshall and the ladies' group had been a big help, lending their ears on more than one occasion, listening to her fears, worries and concerns and offering support and advice when she asked for it. Talking with her new friends had helped and being at Pine Creek Farm seemed to help even more.

A few weeks ago, she'd taken up joining Liam by the firepit after dinner once she'd helped Gayle settle into bed for the night. It was warmer now, but Liam still built a fire, and the spring breeze was just right to make it comfortable and pleasant. Sometimes they talked, but most nights they sat in a comfortable silence and Liam would tip his head back and close his eyes as though in deep thought or prayer.

It hadn't taken her long to do the same, and she found it was easy to talk to God in that space—to look up at the stars, listen to the rhythmic crackle of the fire and chorus of toads and crickets by the pond and listen for God's guidance.

She'd grown to love it here.

Her stomach growled and she smiled, then glanced at Gayle. "I think Oliver's hungry. How about you? Do you have an appetite today?"

Gayle stood slowly, leaning on Mallory's supportive arm, then brushed the dirt off her hands. "I'm thirsty. Do we have any lemonade?"

Mallory nodded. "I made a fresh batch last night." She placed her palm on the ground and, leaning to one side, she pushed herself to her knees then feet and brushed the soil off her hands as well. "How about we take a quick break?" She began walking toward the front steps. "I'll pour us both some lemonade and we'll sit on the porch for a while then—"

Another pain—a sharp one—tore through her, hardening her belly and streaking down her back. Gasping, she doubled over and stumbled forward, managing to grab the porch rail to prevent herself from falling.

"Miss?" Gayle's voice drew closer. "Are you okay?"

Oh no, oh no, oh no—

She still had nine days to prepare. Nine more days!

"Excuse me, miss," Gayle said again, touching her back gently. "Are you okay?"

The pain subsided slightly and Mallory straightened slowly. She turned and summoned a smile. "Yes." Her voice trembled. "But I think I'm in labor."

Gayle gasped, her eyes darting toward Mallory's belly. "My goodness! A baby," she said, as though noticing Mallory's swollen belly for the first time. "You're going to have a baby."

Mallory nodded, dragged in a deep breath and left the porch rail, taking several careful steps across the front lawn. Thankfully, the horses were still in view and Liam was still astride Sugar at the front of the pack.

"Liam!" Mallory waved her arms in the air and shouted again. "Liam!"

Sugar snorted and raised her head as Liam turned in Mallory's direction. He peered across the grounds at her as she called for him again then, sensing the urgency in her tone, urged Sugar into a gallop and raced across the lawn. He halted Sugar several feet away, dismounted and jogged over.

"What is it?" Concern suffused his expression. "Is it Oliver?"

Another painful contraction swept through Mallory and she bent forward, propped her hands on her knees and groaned softly, "Yes."

I do want you, Oliver. I truly do. I'm just—

"Mallory?" Dr. Harper's face slowly swam into focus. "Mallory, I know you're exhausted and I know this is tough, but I need you to start pushing."

Pain ripped through Mallory, arching her back. She shoved her head back against a pillow, opened her eyes and stared up at the ceiling.

Let go, or it'll be worse.

She thrashed her head from side to side at the memory of Trevor's voice then blinked hard and struggled to focus on her surroundings. There was one chair beside the bed, a monitor that beeped, two women dressed in blue scrubs and Dr. Harper sat at the foot of her bed.

Hospital. She was in the hospital. And in labor.

Sweat streamed down her cheek, dripped off her chin and splashed onto her collarbone. *I do want you, Oliver. I do, I'm just sca—*

"Mallory." Drs. Harper's voice was authoritative now. "You've got to listen to me, Mallory. I need you to push."

How had she gotten here?

Liam's face, his hazel eyes worried and apprehensive, floated into her mind. Oh, that's right. He'd gotten off a horse and driven her to the hospital.

Pain tore through her belly and she groaned. What was the horse's name? The pretty brown one?

Sugar. Her name was Sugar.

Let go, or it'll be worse.

"Push, Mallory."

I want you, Oliver. She bit her lip, the taste of blood hitting her tongue. *I'm just terrified. And I need—*

"Mallo—"

"Liam." She opened her mouth wider, sucked in a strong breath and whispered brokenly, "Please get Liam."

Liam stood by a window in the waiting room of the hospital in Pine Creek. It was dark outside, after midnight, and he'd never been more scared in his life.

"It's been over twelve hours," he said, pressing his cell phone closer to his cheek. "No one's come out to give me an update in over two hours now. Is that normal?"

"It's okay, Liam," Jessie said on the other end of the line. "These things take time."

Her words were low and slow as though she were still rousing from a deep sleep. He had hated to call her this time of night, but his anxiety had gotten the best of him.

"I'm sorry for waking you," he said for the third time during that conversation. "And I hope I didn't wake the kids."

"I told you not to worry about that. Ava and the boys are still sleeping soundly," she reassured him. "Is anyone there with you?"

"No. I was in the middle of a trail ride when it started. It all happened so fast. One of the hands stayed with Mom while I drove Mallory to the hospital. I called Pam once I got here and asked if she and the ladies would take turns staying with Mom until we were able to come home."

Home. How sweet that word sounded right now. And how much he wanted to whisk Mallory and Oliver out of the hospital and back to Pine Creek Farm where he could look over them, ensuring they were safe and settled.

But Oliver would have to arrive first, and from the way things were looking, that could take quite a while.

"It wouldn't be so bad if I could see her," he said. His voice sounded rough. Almost unrecognizable to his own ears. "The last time I saw her was when I helped her into a wheelchair and they wheeled her back to a room. I haven't seen or spoken to her since."

"Take that as a positive," Jessie said. "If you haven't heard anything negative and she hasn't been asking for you, then things must be progressing rather well. It takes a lot of work to get a new baby in the world. Try to stay calm and give it time."

Liam dragged his hand over his face. "I can't help but worry. She was in so much pain. You should've seen her face."

"I know," Jessie said gently. "But pain is part of the package and Mallory's tough. I'm sure you've noticed that by now."

He had. Over the past couple of months, he'd worked closely with Mallory every day at Pine Creek Farm, cooking breakfast with her in the morning, helping her with laundry for the guest bedrooms each evening and assisting with Gayle whenever he had the opportunity to break free from work. Mallory had grown more relaxed around him and had even taken to visiting the stable every evening to pet Sugar, check on Miss Priss then walk with him to the firepit and sit under the stars until her eyes grew heavy and she retired to her room for the night.

Those evenings were Liam's favorite part of each day. Sitting beneath the night sky in peaceful silence beside Mallory had been a balm to his soul. It was easy to think and pray, sitting there beside her. And she seemed to enjoy doing the same.

He couldn't help but notice, as time had passed, that Oliver had grown, increasing the swell of Mallory's belly and causing her to move a bit slower each day. He encouraged her as much as he could to rest as often as possible, and he'd been glad to know that she had begun taking naps in the afternoon when Gayle did.

"Her ankles have been really swollen," he said. "She's been wearing flip-flops since the weather got warm and I've noticed it a lot more lately. She gets tired so fast. She sleeps almost as much as Mom does now in the afternoons. Do you think that meant there was something wrong—"

"No," Jessie said firmly. "Not at all. All of that is absolutely normal for a pregnancy." She grew quiet then asked, "You've gotten to know Mallory rather well these past couple of months haven't you?"

"Yes." He stared out the window, his shoulders tensing, feeling as though he knew what she would say next.

"This new baby will change things a lot," Jessie said.

He shoved his free hand in his pocket and continued staring out the window. "I know."

"You'll need extra help with Gayle while Mallory recovers. Holt won't mind if I come down for a couple weeks and help—"

"No." That came out harsher than he meant. He cleared his throat and tried for a softer tone. "We'll be okay. The ladies' group from my church has offered to help in any way we need them to. They'll be able to stay with Gayle for the days that Mallory needs to rest."

"Well, if you change your mi—"

"I won't," he said gently but firmly. "But thank you for the offer, Jessie."

He appreciated it. He truly did. But he knew what he'd be in for if Jessie made the drive down to Pine Creek Farm and settled in for a couple of weeks. She'd watch him close, looking for signs that he'd grown attached to Mallory and she would, no doubt, find them.

No matter how hard he'd tried to keep his distance— and he *had* tried—he'd been unable to keep Mallory from slipping into his heart. Pine Creek Farm was completely different with her there. Every morning, he had something to look forward to. He knew, without fail, that she would emerge from upstairs, join him in the kitchen and return his smile. Inevitably, they would bump into each other at least once in the kitchen while cooking breakfast and she'd laugh and say sorry for the thousandth time.

He loved her laugh. He loved…so much about her.

Love. What a surprising notion. He'd never been in love before. Was this what it felt like? Did it always sneak up unexpectedly then take hold, refusing to be ignored? He hadn't expected falling in love to be so quiet, so peaceful and so quick.

Maybe it wasn't love. Maybe it was something else… but what?

He and Mallory had become friends—the very best of friends. But what he felt for her went far beyond that. The admiration in her gaze when she looked at him, the cheerful sound of her laugh and her dedication to caring for Gayle—supporting his mom in every way possible—had taken him in.

It was, he admitted ruefully, impossible to imagine what Pine Creek Farm might be like were Mallory to leave.

"The offer stands," Jessie said. "If you or Mallory need me, I'm just a phone call away."

Liam, worried and exhausted, dragged in a deep breath. "Thank you. I really mean that."

"I know. You'll call me when the baby comes?"

Liam smiled at the reminder that there was something precious at the end of all this worry and pain. "Yes. I'll be sure to—"

"Liam Williams?"

He spun around at the sound of his name, finding a nurse, clad in blue scrubs, standing in the doorway of the waiting room. She looked at him expectantly.

"I'm sorry, I gotta go, Jessie." He ended the call, shoved his phone in his back pocket then walked across the room. "What is it? Is Mallory okay?"

The nurse pulled her mask down below her chin. "I need you to come back with me, if you don't mind?"

He froze, his heart thundering against his ribs. "The baby, is he—"

"He isn't here yet," the nurse said, propping the door open and motioning for Liam to precede her. "But I think Mallory might need your help. She's asking for you."

That was all she had to say.

Liam took swift strides down the hallway, waiting impatiently for the nurse to catch up and direct him to the right room. When he entered, his gaze darted around the figures standing around the bed, then homed in on Mallory's face.

She looked back at him, her cheeks red and fear in her eyes. "Liam?"

He moved quickly, edging between two nurses, then dragged a chair close to the bed and sat down. "How is she?" he asked the doctor, his eyes still glued to Mallory's.

"She's fine," Dr. Harper said. "But we need her to start pushing. I think she needs some reassurance and extra support."

Liam nodded and scooted closer to the bed. "Tell me what I can do to help, Mallory," he whispered. "Just say the word and I'll do it."

Her hand lifted, her fingers grasping at empty air until they fumbled over his forearm where it lay on the chair's armrest. She closed her hand around his and squeezed tightly.

He stilled, the warm feel of her soft hand against his catching him off guard.

"I'm scared," she whispered.

Immediately, he turned his hand over, weaving his fingers between hers, and leaned close, whispering back, "I know. I'm here."

"Mallory," Dr. Harper prompted from the foot of the bed, "you've got to push now. We've put this off long enough."

Mallory closed her eyes and grimaced. A fresh bead of sweat rolled over her temple and into the damp hair at her temples.

"Mallory?" Dr. Harper said again. "You have to—"

"I'm too scared, Liam." Mallory shook her head, her hair rustling against the pillow. "So scared."

There was a familiar tremor in her voice. The same one he remembered hearing on the day they'd first met at Hummingbird Haven, when she'd spoken of her past…and her ex-husband.

He leaned his elbows onto the bed, lifted their joined hands and urged her eyes to meet his. "Then scream, Mallory. Scream all you like. Just let it out."

She opened her eyes and stared back at him, then, breathing heavily, opened her mouth and yelled, the sound one of anguish, fear and pain.

Liam winced as the keening wail left her lips. It broke his heart just a bit more.

"Mallory, I know you're in pain," Dr. Harper said. "But if you're yelling and making noise, you're not really pushing. I need you to push."

"She will," Liam said firmly, scooting even closer. He brushed Mallory's damp bangs from her forehead, waited until she was silent and met his eyes again. "Now, push," he urged. "After you push, you can scream again. Scream all you want in between, so long as you push."

Her hand tightened around his then she lifted onto her elbows and grew silent, her expression twisting in pain.

"Good, Mallory," Dr. Harper soothed. "That's good. Keep that up."

The pattern continued for several more minutes as Mallory's screams and Dr. Harper's vocal urgings as Mallory pushed filled the room. But soon, another cry sounded. It was the sweetest one Liam had ever heard.

"You did it," Dr. Harper said, smiling at Mallory. "You delivered a beautiful baby boy."

There was a flurry of movement in the room as Dr. Harper passed the infant to the nurses and they went to work, cleaning the infant up and taking initial measurements.

Liam looked down at Mallory and smiled gently as her eyelids, pink and heavy, drooped low. She was exhausted. "Hey," he said, smoothing his thumb over her damp brow. "You did it, Mallory."

Her eyes closed and she didn't answer. But her mouth parted and her breaths grew slower and even.

"Liam?"

He glanced over his shoulder at a nurse who held Oliver, clean and swaddled, in her arms. "Would you like to give Mallory her baby?"

He squeezed Mallory's hand once more then stood slowly, walked over to the nurse and held out his arms.

She placed Oliver in his open embrace, the baby's slight weight settling perfectly into the crook of his elbow. Liam looked down and smiled, savoring the moment. His heart overflowed and he blinked back hot tears then, after gaining his composure, carefully returned to his chair, leaned forward and settled Oliver onto Mallory's chest, supporting him with both hands.

"Mallory?" Her eyes fluttered open at the feel of Oliver against her chest. "Here he is."

She tipped her head down, her eyes roving over Oliver's face. She pulled back the blanket a tiny bit, then pressed one fingertip against Oliver's palm and watched as his tiny fingers curled around her finger.

"He has your eyes," Liam whispered, watching as Oliver's wide gaze fixed on Mallory's face. "And he has your nose. He's the most perfect baby I've ever seen."

Mallory continued staring down at the baby then she smiled, a tired but happy smile as she whispered, "Oliver. My sweet Ollie."

The tenderness in her voice was unmistakable and Liam sagged against the mattress beneath the weight of the day. They were beautiful. Both of them. And if he had a choice, he'd stay right there, in that very moment, forever.

"Liam?" He blinked hard against a fresh surge of tears and looked at Mallory again. She reached out, cupped his jaw and drifted her thumb over his stubbled cheek. "Thank you."

You were born today, Oliver.

It was scarier than I anticipated, bringing you into the world, but I had some help. I asked for Liam and he came. He held my hand through it all and he was the first to hold you.

I wish I could tell you how I felt when he placed you in my arms, but there aren't words for it. Not for what I was feeling.

How can I describe how it felt to have you snuggle against my chest—a tiny piece of me—the sweetest, most innocent little boy in the world? How can I tell you how it felt to look into eyes that were exactly like mine? To know that you're a part of me and that I'm a part of you?

What a miracle you are! What a beautiful gift from God.

I fell in love with you, right then and there. You stole my heart, Oliver. And you'll have it forever.

Chapter Eight

⟋⟍

Three days later, Mallory brought Oliver home.

She sat in the passenger seat of Liam's truck, sitting sideways and smiling at Oliver's reflection in a small mirror that Liam had mounted to the back window of the truck's cab.

"How's he doing back there?" Liam asked, slowing the truck as they neared the turn to the driveway of Pine Creek Farm.

Mallory squirmed to the side a bit more and sighed. "He's perfect. Just like you said."

Oliver was fast asleep in his rear-facing car seat, strapped safely inside and covered with a light but cozy blanket. His hair, thick for an infant, curled adorably at the ends. His lush lashes rested against his healthy, flushed cheeks and his small mouth was parted. If she leaned back far enough and listened hard, she could just hear the rhythmic whisper of his breathing.

"I can't wait to get him home and settled in the nursery," she said, looking at Liam.

Pam and the rest of the ladies had worked hard over the past couple of months, helping Mallory plan, shop and gather materials to bring their vision for Oliver's nursery to life. They weren't the only ones though. Liam had been the one to paint the walls, taking care to get the trim just right, and being cautious about keeping the wood floors unstained and gleaming.

Barbara had come through as well. She had a friend in a local store in downtown Pine Creek who had a plethora of rugs in various colors and patterns for every nursery theme. And there had been so many blankets—blankets of all materials and styles—that Mallory had found several to match the shade of blue they'd chosen for the nursery.

Oliver's nursery was perfect and so many loving people—including Liam—had gone to a lot of trouble to make it so.

Liam glanced at her briefly and smiled. "He's gonna love it."

Mallory grinned. "He's gonna love Gayle, too."

Gayle often forgot that Mallory was having a baby, but each time she noticed, the first thing she said was that she couldn't wait to hold the baby. Oh, she'd be thrilled when Oliver arrived home!

"She's been waiting a long time to get her hands on Oliver," Liam said as he slowed the truck even more and turned right onto the long driveway leading to Pine Creek Farm.

Mallory allowed her gaze to linger on his profile, tracing the strong, stubbled curve of his jaw with her eyes and admiring his handsome features. Three days ago, she'd been fond of him, but now, after experiencing his strength and encouragement in the hospital during labor and the days after, she was afraid he'd stolen her heart completely.

Her breath caught at the thought, and she faced the road ahead as well.

It wouldn't do to jump to conclusions right now. She'd been through a lot over the past three days, so it was understandable and expected that her emotions were intense and unpredictable at times. It'd be easy to attach the tenderness, excitement and affection that filled her heart for Oliver to Liam as well. After all, he'd been there for her during the most challenging time of her life.

After he'd placed Oliver in her arms, Liam had stayed by her side in the hospital room as they'd counted Oliver's fingers and toes, and discussed how beautiful he was until the nurses took him to the nursery for the evening.

Soon after, Mallory had fallen asleep, her body exhausted and sore. She'd slept soundly and when she'd awoken, Liam had still been there.

She smiled as she recalled the image. He'd been sitting in the chair beside the bed, his long legs sprawled out, his jaw stubbled as it was now, and his head propped against the headrest of the chair at an odd angle. But when he'd stirred and opened his eyes, then looked into her own, he'd smiled brighter than she'd ever seen him smile before and his sleepy eyes had filled with joy.

Her heart had swelled. Despite a different location, their morning routine had only changed in one respect. Just as at Pine Creek Farm, Liam's smile was the first thing she saw every morning of her hospital stay. But rather than following him to the kitchen to cook breakfast, breakfast had been delivered to her and Liam by hospital staff.

"Pam called me as I was bringing the truck around to pick you and Oliver up at the front entrance of the hospital," Liam said now. "She and the ladies' group wanted to be there when you and Oliver arrived home this afternoon."

Home. A beautiful word and one she was surprised to find she preferred to use for Pine Creek Farm. She pressed her palm against her chest as she glanced to the left and right of the driveway as Liam drove, admiring the full blooms on the magnolia trees that towered above them.

The afternoon sun was bright, the fields were green and the main house, with its white siding and large front porch, completed the picturesque scene.

Pine Creek Farm was perfect. As perfect as Oliver.

Mallory closed her eyes for a moment and said a silent prayer of thanks for the new baby, generous friends and the beautiful place to lay her head. She couldn't imagine anyone not feeling at home at Pine Creek Farm and it'd feel even more welcoming today, what with the ladies' group and Gayle coming to welcome—

"Did Pam mention how Gayle was doing?" Mallory asked.

She hoped her absence and the subsequent lack of predictability to each day hadn't upset Gayle too much. Mallory had asked, while she was in the hospital, if Liam might bring Gayle to visit, but Liam had thought it best not to disrupt or confuse her anymore. He said the change in routine had already upset her. Instead, he'd arranged for Pam and the other ladies to stay with her, keeping her routine in much the same way as Mallory usually did and helping with chores and assisting guests until they could return home.

"Pam said she had a great breakfast and a good lunch but that she was getting a bit tired," Liam said. "I'm glad they released you when they did, because I think we just might make it inside before it's time for her nap."

"That's it then," Mallory said, smiling. "Gayle is the first on Oliver's guest list."

She couldn't wait to see Gayle's face when she held Oliver for the first time.

When they reached the end of the driveway, Liam parked the truck beside several vehicles that were already parked in front of the house. "I see the ladies' group are already here. You should probably expect a slightly over-the-top welcome."

Mallory laughed. "That's okay. I think Oliver has earned some extra attention."

Liam hopped out of the truck first, indicating for Mallory to wait until he rounded the truck and opened her door. He helped her out then unbuckled Oliver from his car seat and carefully, oh so carefully, cradled Oliver against his broad chest as he lifted him out of the car seat and placed him in Mallory's waiting arms. His blunt fingertips brushed her forearms as he released Oliver and she suppressed a wave of affection for him, hiding the heat in her cheeks by ducking her head and focusing on Oliver's sleeping face.

"It's good he's still sleeping," Mallory said softly. "He'll wake up, ready to eat soon, and cry for all he's worth. While he's sleeping, Gayle will get to meet him when he's at his most peaceful."

Liam gently brushed the back of his knuckles over Oliver's downy hair. "Peaceful or not, he's at his best every moment of the day."

Tenderness flooded Mallory's chest at the loving gaze Liam bestowed on Oliver. What would it be like to have him look at her like that? What might it feel like to be loved by Liam? To feel safe, protected and supported by him as a wife? It was something she had begun to wonder about more and more about each day.

They walked across the front lawn, climbed the front porch steps and went inside. Liam hovered by Mallory's side every step of the way, opening the front door and cradling her hand with his beneath Oliver's head as she walked slowly into the living room.

"Oh, there they are!" Peggy, seated in a living room chair, sprang to her feet and walked briskly across the room to look down at baby Oliver. "He's precious, Mallory. Just precious."

Wendy, Barbara and Cherie Ann were there as well. They rushed over and each of them took their turn gazing with adoration at Oliver, asking questions about his weight and height, and inquiring about Mallory's health.

"We're both completely healthy," Mallory said, smoothing her fingertips over the back of Oliver's hand as he slept.

A sense of pride moved through her as she looked down at him. He was, without a doubt, the most precious person in her life.

"Mallory did an excellent job getting Oliver into the world safely," Liam said.

Mallory looked up at him then, the affection in his gaze, so similar to how he looked at Oliver, making her heart turn over in her chest. "I can't take all the credit," she said softly. "I did have some help." She looked at the other women, who had leaned in, their wide, curious eyes moving from Liam to Mallory then back. "Liam stayed with me during labor. He held my hand and gave me a good pep talk. I don't think I'd have made it without him."

Pam was the first to speak, a slow smile curving her lips as she whispered, "How wonderful."

"Liam was the first to hold Oliver," Mallory added.

"And it's our turn now, right?" Barbara asked, clapping her hands together in glee.

Mallory laughed. "Soon enough. But Oliver already has someone very special waiting for him." She peered past the ladies and met Gayle's gaze across the room from where she sat on the sofa. "Gayle? Oliver's finally here to meet you."

Gayle lifted her head and looked at Mallory. Her eyes were heavy with fatigue but at the sight of the bundle in

Mallory's arms, her expression brightened. She smiled and spread her arms wide. "My grandbaby?"

Mallory eased between the women, walked across the room and sat on the couch beside Gayle. "Yes. This is Oliver."

Gayle looked down at him and her eyes filled with tears. "He's beautiful," she whispered.

"Would you like to hold him?" Mallory asked.

At her eager nod, Mallory scooted closer and eased Oliver into Gayle's arms.

Liam was there in an instant, kneeling by Gayle's side and cupping her delicate hands with his own as she cradled Oliver against her chest. "You're a pro at this, Mom," he said softly as he tucked a wayward strand of gray hair behind her ear.

Gayle continued looking down at Oliver. "I've had my own you know," she said, smoothing one finger over the back of Oliver's hand. "His name was Holt." Tears spilled over her cheeks as she whispered, "Holt. The sweetest son in the world."

Mallory stilled, her gaze moving to Liam.

He continued to kneel by Gayle's side and murmur encouraging words, but some of the joy had faded from his eyes.

Later that night, when darkness had settled over Pine Creek Farm, the stars had emerged and a full moon glowed bright above, Liam carried two thick logs in his arms to the firepit behind the main house. He stacked them on top of another log that had not quite burned completely several nights before, shoved a hunk of kindling in between them and lit a match.

As the logs began to catch fire, he walked over to the two Adirondack chairs and fluffed up a pillow he had placed in one hours earlier. He also adjusted the light blanket he'd draped over the armrest of the chair. It was warm out but there was a nice breeze in the evening air. If Mallory decided to join him, the pillow might make the hard Adirondack chair more comfortable against her back and the light blanket would keep her bare legs warm.

That was, if she decided to join him.

He glanced over his shoulder at the main house. Most of the windows were dark except for a couple lights in two downstairs guest rooms, and the soft yellow glow of porch lights pooled onto the back deck of the house. By now Mallory would be sitting by Gayle's bedside, reading to her from the Bible and helping her drift off to sleep as usual. Only, tonight there was something different in the routine.

Liam grinned. Oliver was here.

After Pam and the rest of the ladies had taken turns holding Oliver, cooing at him and complimenting Mallory, Oliver had woken and cried his little heart out, demanding to be fed. Mallory had carried Oliver upstairs to the nursery and Pam and the ladies had said their goodbyes, excused themselves and left for the afternoon.

The thought of the nursery made him chuckle. Throughout the room, happy teddy bears had taken over.

Mallory and the ladies had done an excellent job decorating over the past couple of months. He had helped by painting the walls a soft shade of blue that matched the plush teddy bear Mallory had tucked onto a large, comfortable rocking chair that she'd placed in the room. Liam had put together a crib and changing table as well, following Mallory's direction as to which corner of the room to position each.

Teddy bears seem to have been the theme Mallory and the ladies had adopted for the nursery. There were colorful rugs with images of dancing bears of every shape and size, the sheets on the mattress and the crib were decorated the same and a mobile hanging over the crib was adorned with several smiling teddy bears that spun, dipped and twirled when the mobile was powered on.

Unable to resist, Liam had stopped by the nursery door and knocked after helping Gayle settle for a nap earlier that afternoon, then waited for Mallory to invite him in.

She had but after opening the door, he'd been hesitant to interrupt. Instead, he'd stood in the doorway on the threshold, remaining silent as Mallory, seated in the rocking chair, rocked Oliver in her arms as she burped him. Soon after, he'd slipped quietly away and returned to his chores, smiling ear to ear, already looking forward to seeing them both again at dinner.

When he knocked off work for the day and returned to the main house to prepare dinner, he discovered that the ladies' group had stocked the fridge and freezer full of casseroles, soups and side dishes. But a glazed ham caught his eye and he'd warmed it up in the oven, along with two side dishes and fresh bread, then set the table.

The delectable aroma had filled the house and, as expected, Mallory and Gayle had joined him at the dining table with eager smiles and baby Oliver had wiggled in his bassinet beside Mallory, his brief cries and sniffles mingling with the clink of their utensils against the plates.

Still smiling, Liam sat in his chair, leaned his head against the headrest and closed his eyes. How different the house had felt then, surrounded by those he loved.

Love—there was that word again. What else could he call it? The swell of tenderness within his chest grew more and more each day he spent with Mallory and Oliver. He couldn't remember how the house had sounded and felt without Mallory's presence and now he knew he'd find it hard to envision what it would be like without Mallory and Oliver…or his mother.

A heavy sigh left him, and he opened his eyes and gazed at the stars as they glittered overhead. His mom had cried this afternoon when she'd held Oliver and her tears had continued long after Mallory had removed Oliver from her arms and carried the baby upstairs. He'd sat with Gayle for some time, handing her fresh tissues, trying to distract her with news about the farm and the new guests that had arrived, but nothing had seemed to help.

He rubbed his forehead, his head aching. Her reaction to holding Oliver was another sign, another symptom of her progressing dementia. Her moods had become erratic and she had difficulty orienting herself to place and time. Only one name still remained, unchanged, in her mind, familiar and adored.

Holt.

Liam didn't resent that she remembered his brother—not at all. He loved Holt and he loved his mother, and knowing that she remembered at least one of her sons was a comfort. That knowledge would, hopefully, ease her mind a bit. Holt was someone she could reflect on when she was most afraid. She could seek refuge there, in his memory, in the reminder of someone familiar.

But despite this, Liam couldn't prevent the hurt that arose within him each time she said his brother's name and neglected to say his own. Though logically, he knew it to be untrue, he felt as though he'd never existed in her world. As though every memory of him had been erased from her mind and heart, never to return again.

And one day—more than likely sooner rather than later—he would lose her altogether.

His throat tightened and he swallowed hard, holding tears at bay. He wouldn't dwell on that now. He wouldn't think of it. The notion was too painful to bear.

"Mind if I join you?"

Almost immediately, his grief subsided as he smiled at the familiar voice.

He stood and faced Mallory as she strolled toward the fire pit, her brows raised. "You know you have a permanent invitation." He motioned toward the chair beside his own. "I brought a pillow out for you." Rounding the chair, he waited until she sat down then adjusted the pillow behind her lower back. "How's that?"

"Wonderful," she said, placing a baby monitor she held on the armrest and closing her eyes. "Thank you."

"You're welcome," he said. "It's warm but there's a cool breeze that's steady." He picked up the blanket and draped it over her knees. "This'll keep your legs warm."

"You've thought of everything," she said, smiling up at him. "But I suppose I should be used to that. You always think of others before yourself."

He didn't quite know how to react, but he knew what he wanted to do. He wanted to lean down, nuzzle his cheek against hers, breathe in her sweet scent and hug her close. He wanted to brush her soft mouth with his and savor the sight of her beautiful eyes up close.

But that wouldn't do.

Instead, he shrugged. "You do exactly the same for me and Mom." He grinned. "And Oliver."

Her eyes closed briefly at the mention of her son's name, her cheeks blushing. "He is perfect, isn't he? Just like you said."

"Yes."

"I don't know that either one of us would've pulled

through as well as we did if you hadn't been in the room with me," she added. "I don't think I've ever thanked you properly—"

"You've thanked me," he said, returning to his chair and sitting. "Besides, it wasn't so much a favor to you as it was a comfort to me. I felt better being in the delivery room, being able to see you, rather than sitting in the waiting room wondering how you and Oliver were faring."

She dipped her head, the pretty blush spreading down her neck, and her long wavy hair slipped over one shoulder. "The labor was a bit more overwhelming than I expected," she said softly. "It brought up so many things for me. Memories I didn't want and feelings I thought I had buried a long time ago."

He remained silent, studying the graceful curve of her cheek beneath the moonlight.

"They've quieted down now," she whispered tentatively. "The memories. Something's changed since I had Oliver. The moment I held him, I felt it. I was relieved that he looked like me instead of Tr—" She stopped speaking and looked away for a moment before facing him again. "But that wasn't the only reason. Seeing Oliver, holding him for the first time, I never knew you could love someone so much, so quickly."

Liam smiled. "You're going to be a great mother."

"Do you think so?" she asked.

"I know so," he said softly. "You already are."

"He's sleeping now." She glanced at the baby monitor and turned up the sound, smiling at Liam as Oliver's soft, rhythmic breaths emitted from the speaker. Snuggling more comfortably against the pillow behind her back, she continued, "It takes so little to make him happy that sometimes I think he's going to be a better son than I'll be a mother."

Liam's smile faded and he looked up again, focusing on the stars.

After a few minutes, Mallory asked, "What are you thinking about?"

He looked at the moon. Studied the light as it pooled over the leaves in the tops of the trees. "I'm wondering if I've been that for my mom."

"Been what?"

"A good son."

"Of course you have," she said. "You've been a great one. You're a wonderful man, Liam, and you take such good care of her."

He rolled his head to the side and met her eyes. "Then why doesn't she remember me?"

Mallory frowned. Her eyes darkened with sadness as she examined his expression.

After a moment, she reached out and placed her hand over his, where it lay on the armrest of his chair. She wove her fingers between his and squeezed gently. "In her heart, she remembers."

Liam turned his attention to the night sky again, but silently savored the warm press of Mallory's palm against his own. "I wish I could believe that."

They sat in silence for a while, gazing at the stars, listening to the frogs and crickets croak and chirp near the pond, and relishing the gentle breeze as it swept across the grounds.

Before long, Liam's eyes grew heavy, and he struggled to keep them open. He must've drifted off at some point, because a rustle of movement and light touch on his right forearm prompted him back to awareness.

"In her heart," Mallory whispered near his ear, "she remembers. You're not the kind of man a woman could forget."

Before he could respond, her lips brushed his cheek in the softest of kisses then she drew away, the warmth of her presence fading as she stood and walked away. "Good night, Liam."

I brought you home today, Oliver.

Maybe I shouldn't call Pine Creek Farm our home. After all, I only came here for a job. I came here hoping to start over and make a new life for us both somewhere else in the future.

But this place, you see, has begun to feel like home. Especially now that you're here, living under this roof with me. You, Gayle...and Liam.

Mallory touched her lips. It was still there, the lingering sensation of having kissed Liam, however briefly. His cheek had been warm and stubbled, and his distinctive scent had filled her senses, mingling with the faint smoke of the fire and the scent of spring wildflowers that drifted on the air surrounding them. It had felt like...

"Home," she whispered. Then began writing again.

Pine Creek Farm feels like home, Oliver. And Gayle and Liam feel like family.

I wish we could stay here forever.

Chapter Nine

Spring gave way to summer at Pine Creek Farm. Full, colorful blooms opened on the petunias Mallory and Gayle had planted around the main house, dancing on the summer breeze as though in cheerful welcome to whoever approached the front steps. The sprawling fields filled in with thick, healthy grass, hummingbirds vibrated around feeders Mallory and Gayle had filled with sugar water and hung on the front porch and occasionally—if Mallory sat outside with Gayle at just the right time of day—they'd catch sight of wild rabbits springing stealthily across the front lawn.

The magnolia trees, every branch adorned with bountiful blooms and strong leaves, stood proud and elegant along both sides of the driveway. Pine Creek Farm was bursting at the seams with vibrant summer colors, the sweet scent of honeysuckle and relaxed guests.

And on June 11, Oliver turned three months old.

"Good job, sweet boy. Now, try again."

Mallory, sitting on a blanket in the front yard in preparation for a picnic, smiled as Gayle lifted a blue teething ring toward Oliver. Oliver, seated comfortably in a soft bouncer between Gayle and Mallory, reached out with both hands, his fingers opening and closing as he attempted to grasp the teething ring.

"Keep going, my love," Mallory said, grinning. "You've almost got it."

At the sound of her voice, Oliver swiveled his head to the side. When his big brown eyes met hers, he smiled.

Mallory laughed, leaned over and kissed the brown curls that waved onto his forehead. It wasn't his first smile—not by a long shot—but she couldn't help but be surprised and delighted at the sight of every smile that curved his mouth.

He'd grown so much over the past three months. He ate and slept on a regular schedule now, sleeping through the night for at least five to seven hours. And, best of all, he recognized her face. His expression lit up every time she walked into view and Mallory couldn't help but feel a burgeoning sense of pride. She hoped she was a good mother. She tried every day to care for Oliver even better than she had the day before.

"There he goes," Gayle said, laughing. "He got a hold of it. Such a strong boy."

As if pleased with the praise, Oliver shook the teething ring in his hand and chortled, smiling wider.

"And look at those little feet go," Gayle said. "He might be a runner one day."

"That he might." Grinning, Mallory reached out and tickled the bottom of Oliver's bare foot.

Oliver smiled wider and wiggled.

"You're a busy little guy, aren't you?" Mallory teased.

If he wasn't smiling and waving his arms, trying to grab anything that came near him, his little legs were going a mile a minute, his feet pumping in the air wherever he sat or lay, as though testing out their strength and mobility.

"I think you're just excited to be outside again," Mallory said, tickling his toes.

And she couldn't blame him.

It was another beautiful day at Pine Creek Farm. Being early afternoon, the scorching heat of the summer day had not yet arrived. Instead, the air was warm and pleasant—even if it was a bit humid—the sky was clear and the sun bright, and the grounds were bustling with activity as guests strolled about the fields, fished in the pond or rode horses across the front field in a trail ride.

Mallory closed her eyes and inhaled deeply, breathing in a lungful of fresh country air. "Room to breathe," she whispered.

That's what Liam had promised Pine Creek Farm would offer her when he'd offered her the caretaking job. And that's exactly what Pine Creek Farm had delivered.

Liam. Her mouth curved in a dreamy smile as she thought of him. She'd found it increasingly hard not to think of him lately. There'd been no more kisses beside the firepit, or anything else that wasn't well within the confines of friendship. But…she still had the memory of that one soft kiss she'd brushed against his cheek and the warm feel of his hand beneath hers. And every day, as they cooked breakfast in the kitchen, ate lunch together and sat by the firepit at night, Liam had begun feeling even more like family.

Being in his company was easy. Comfortable. There was a peace between them that she'd never experienced with Trevor—or any other man before. She could close her eyes when sitting beside him by the firepit in the evening and feel completely at ease. Her affection for him had intensified and continued to grow a little more every day.

If only she knew how he really felt about her.

He hadn't mentioned the kiss since it happened, and he didn't seem likely to. The morning afterward, he'd greeted her with a smile downstairs as usual, and they'd gone about the day as they had all the days before since her arrival.

But there was something in his eyes now when he looked at her. And, on more than one occasion, she'd caught his gaze lingering on her. When she'd notice him studying her, he'd meet her eyes and smile, gazing just a bit more before he broke eye contact and moved on. Each time, she'd gotten the impression that he had something he wanted to say and a few times, she thought he might actually voice his thoughts.

But that hadn't happened. Whatever secrets Liam had in his mind or heart, he continued to keep them to himself.

"Mind if I join you?"

Mallory shook herself slightly at the sound of his voice and glanced over her shoulder to find him striding across the front lawn in her direction. "You know you have a permanent invitation," she teased, smiling.

He laughed and took his hat off and tossed it onto the edge of the blanket where she and Gayle sat, then sat down beside Mallory. "That's good to know. I noticed earlier that you were carrying one of Pam's baskets out here," he said, nodding at the large straw basket on the edge of the blanket. "I asked one of the hands to lead the trail ride this afternoon so that I could join y'all on the off chance that you might have food in that thing."

Mallory laughed, too. "Then you made a good choice because that's exactly what's in there. It's a beautiful day, the flowers are blooming and we thought you might enjoy a picnic outside."

Or, at least, she hoped so. One constant since the day she'd kissed Liam had been that he had never missed eating lunch with Mallory, Gayle and Oliver. No matter how busy things became at Pine Creek Farm or how many trail ride requests he had to fill for guests, Liam always made time to return to the main house to eat lunch with them, hold Oliver for at least ten minutes and share a laugh or two before returning to work.

"I look forward to seeing this little man every day." Grinning, Liam reached out and held up one finger close enough for Oliver to reach out and grab. Oliver accepted the invitation, his tiny palm wrapping tightly around Liam's finger. "He's getting stronger, isn't he?"

"He's a runner, too," Gayle said. "Look at those feet go."

Glancing down at where Oliver's feet kicked at a steady pace in the bouncer, Liam chuckled. "I think you're right about that, Mom. He never slows down, does he?"

Mallory shook her head. "Nope. He's a busy little guy." She reached behind her and lifted the lid off a cooler, dug around in the ice and withdrew a cold bottle of water. "Need a drink?"

"I'd love one." Liam took the bottle from her, unscrewed the cap then tipped it back, drawing deeply.

He'd gotten a tan over the past couple of months. More than likely, the tan had developed during the long hours of leading trail rides in the afternoon. It suited him. With his blond hair, hazel eyes and sun-kissed skin, he looked healthy, energetic and happy.

Realizing she was staring, Mallory pried her gaze away from Liam, ducked her head then dragged the picnic basket close. "Pam dropped off more barbecue sandwiches this morning when she and Barbara came to visit Oliver. She said she thought you might like them since you and the hands enjoyed them so much last time."

Liam set the water bottle down on the blanket and rubbed his hands together. "Oh, you have no idea how much I want those right now."

Mallory smiled. "Hard morning?"

"Lots of trail rides," he said, accepting a sandwich, wrapped in plastic, as she passed it to him. "All of the guesthouses are rented out and several children arrived with the last two families that checked in. They're old enough to ride but they've never done so before so I had to give them several lessons before we took the horses out today."

"Did they enjoy the ride?" she asked.

Liam nodded as he unwrapped his sandwich. "One of the boys was a natural." He took a bite of his sandwich, chewed then swallowed before saying, "He took off on his own a time or two. I had to chase him down and was scared to death I wouldn't catch him before anything unwelcome occurred. I reminded him several times that horses—even the best of them—can be unpredictable."

"Always the protector," Mallory said softly. It was something she loved most about him.

His eyes met hers and she stilled, heat suffusing her cheeks. A slow smile spread across his face as though he could read her thoughts and knew exactly what she was thinking.

But he didn't know how she truly felt about him, did he? Gracious, she hoped not. She'd been very careful—especially after kissing him—to keep a healthy distance between them. To keep the relationship as it had always been before she'd kissed him—strictly on the level of good friendship.

But behaving like Liam's friend didn't keep her heart from longing to be something more.

"There he goes again," Gayle said, pointing at Oliver. "He caught it the first time I held it out to him."

Oliver kicked his legs in his bouncer and waved a second teething ring in the air with a bright smile as though in triumphant success.

Liam laughed. "Good job, buddy." He glanced at Mallory. "Do you mind if I hold him for a little while?"

She shook her head. "Not at all."

He put his sandwich down, wiped his hands on a napkin then reached out and lifted Oliver from his bouncer. Liam's hands, though big and strong, could not have been more gentle or loving than if he were Oliver's biological father.

The thought sent a wave of longing through Mallory.

"Has he had his lunch yet?" Liam asked, glancing at Mallory again.

She nodded.

"Good." He looked down at Oliver and smiled, drifting his thumb over Oliver's soft curls. "That means we'll have more time to hang out. Whatcha feel like doing today, buddy? Wanna see if we can spot any of those bunnies running around the front yard?"

Oliver cooed again and kicked his legs.

"I'd like to hold him again." Gayle looked at Oliver longingly.

"Well now," Liam said, smiling down at Oliver. "Mamas always come first." He turned to Gayle and handed Oliver to her, making sure Oliver was settled safely within her arms before releasing him. "Take all the time you want, Mom. I need to finish my sandwich anyway."

Oliver, seemingly just as happy in Gayle's arms as in Liam's, continued to coo as Gayle spoke to him.

"You're such a happy boy," Gayle said. "So friendly and easygoing. Nothing seems to ruffle you."

Mallory met Liam's eyes and smiled. He smiled back but there was a lingering sadness shadowing his eyes.

They'd both noticed that Oliver seemed to be the brightest spot in Gayle's day. Over the past week especially, Gayle had begun sleeping later and later every morning and became disoriented much more often. Two days ago, she'd declined Mallory's offer to go outside for the afternoon, which was unlike her. Normally, Gayle loved the outdoors and enjoyed their slow walks down the driveway beneath the magnolia trees.

But lately, that had changed. Her energy was depleted, she seemed less motivated to do anything—especially activities she used to love—and she smiled much less often.

Liam had become worried. Mallory could see it in his face every time he looked at Gayle. He watched her closely more and more every day, asking how she was feeling, if she needed anything and checking with Mallory for any changes—however small—in her behavior.

Mallory could imagine how difficult it must be for him to be unable to slow or stop the decline of his mother's health. Liam always took care of others before himself. It was his nature.

"I had a little boy like you once," Gayle said, gently tapping Oliver's chin.

Liam picked up his bottle of water, drank deeply then resumed eating his sandwich.

"Only," Gayle said, "he had blond hair instead of brown. He had big hazel eyes and the sweetest laugh I've ever heard."

Liam took another bite of his sandwich.

"And when he grew up," Gayle said, "he was tall. So very tall and strong. He took care of me, you know? He took care of the farm, the house, my magnolias. Liam was a perfect son."

Mallory stilled, her eyes darting to Liam.

He paused in the act of drinking water, then lowered his bottle to the blanket and looked at Gayle. "Mom?"

Gayle didn't seem to notice him speak. Instead, she continued looking at Oliver, her smile growing. "I can tell you're going to be like Liam. So loving, so kind. Always giving more than you get. Always doing the right thing."

A sheen of moisture glinted in Liam's eyes beneath the sunlight. He looked at Mallory, his mouth parting, but no sound emerged.

"I hope your little one grows up to be like Liam," Gayle said, looking at Mallory. "He'd be a blessing to you."

Mallory looked at Liam, the joy in his expression stealing her breath. "Yes," she whispered. "I hope, very much, that Oliver grows up to be just like Liam."

They stayed outside for a while, sitting on the blanket, watching Gayle play with Oliver. She never seemed to recognize Liam, who sat beside her, smiling with tears in his eyes, but she continued praising the man named Liam who she remembered as her son.

After a while, Gayle's speech began to slow and her eyelids grew heavy.

"Mom." Liam reached for Oliver. "It's about time for your nap. Why don't we put Oliver back in his bouncer and get you inside and up to your bed? You look tired."

Gayle blinked as Liam lifted Oliver from her arms and settled him back in the bouncer. "Yes," she whispered, as though in a daze. "I am tired."

Mallory rose to her knees. "I'll help you get settled in your ro—"

"That's okay," Liam said, smiling. "Let me do it this time?"

Mallory sat back down. "Of course."

Liam looked at Gayle. "What do you say, Mom? Would you mind if I walk with you inside and help you get settled for your nap? I can read to you for a little while, if you'd like." He winked at Mallory. "My voice may not be as soothing as Mallory's but I'll read to you as long as you'd like."

Gayle nodded. "That'd be fine. Thank you, young man."

Liam stood then bent, cupping his hands under Gayle's arms and helping her stand. He thanked Mallory for lunch then left, leading Gayle up the front porch steps of the main house.

Mallory, tears in her eyes, watched them leave then looked at Oliver, who cooed. "Yeah," she whispered. "I hope you grow up to be just like Liam."

Today had been a good day. No, today had been a great day.

Liam brushed Sugar's back and smiled. The stable was quiet, all the hands having left an hour earlier to knock off for the day, and dusk was settling over Pine Creek Farm. With the sun dipping low in the sky, the hot summer air had cooled to a comfortable temperature and the dying sunlight hit the landscape just right, casting a pink glow across the sky and through the open doors of the stable.

It was as though God had decided to tie a beautiful bow on the gift he'd given him today.

Liam laughed, his heart full. His mother had remembered him. She may not have recognized his face, but she had remembered his name. More than that. She'd described the things she admired most about him. There had been love in her words—the emotion had gentled every syllable—and the expression on her face as she'd looked down at Oliver in her arms had been the same expression she'd had when she'd looked at him as a child.

He could remember those summer days of childhood and early teenage years clearly. The times during summer when he and Holt would go down to the pond, fish for hours, then haul their catch back up to the main house.

Their mom had always been waiting for them in the rocking chair on the front porch, watching the sun set and waiting for their silhouetted figures to emerge over the hill. And when he and Holt had reached the front steps, a mouth-watering aroma had drifted from the kitchen and through the screen door, wafting over the front steps.

Holt had always dropped his cooler of fish outside, kissed their mom's cheek then run inside to start eating the dinner she always had waiting for them. Liam, on the other hand, had taken both of their fish hauls to the sink at the back of the house and had cleaned and packed them in ice before coming inside to eat his dinner.

When he arrived, his mother would stand from the dining room table, walk across the room and wrap her arms around him. He could remember her kissing his cheek, smiling softly and saying, "My sweet Liam. Always doing the right thing."

He'd been loved—Liam blinked back happy tears—and remembered.

That thought alone was enough to fill his heart with joy. The knowledge that his mother, despite her illness, still cherished some memory of him safely in her heart. Mallory had been sure of it. What was it she had whispered near his ear when she'd kissed him all those weeks ago?

In her heart, she remembers. You're not the kind of man a woman could forget.

He closed his eyes and smiled wider, saying a brief, silent prayer of thanks for all of the blessings God had given him. And there had been so very many blessings lately.

A plaintive meow sounded behind him.

Liam stopped brushing Sugar and glanced over his shoulder to find Miss Priss sitting nearby.

She stared up at him, her wide, intimidating eyes unblinking.

"So, what's up?" Liam asked. "Did you come to visit me or are you looking for Mallory?"

It had to be the latter. The cat had grown quite fond of Mallory. It followed her around whenever she took Gayle for a walk across the grounds and lingered nearby when she rocked Oliver on the front porch.

The cat stared at him for a moment longer then blinked slowly, stretched out on its side then rolled over onto its back, exposing its furry belly.

Liam raised his brows. "Oh, you don't think I'm gonna fall for that, do you?"

Miss Priss stared at him.

"If I pet you," he asked, "you're gonna bite me, right? Maybe rip my arm off?"

Miss Priss blinked slow again then wiggled. The feline looked far too adorable in light of the menacing personality she harbored.

"All right," Liam said softly, lowering to his haunches. "I'll give you a chance. Just…be kind."

Hesitantly, he lifted his hand and reached out, steering clear of Miss Priss's belly—he was nowhere near brave enough to chance petting her there—and touched her head, stroking her fur ever so slightly.

Miss Priss remained still, then her eyes slowly closed and she nudged his hand with her nose.

"Will you look at that?" Liam said, smiling. "I'm growing on you, am I?"

As if in response, Miss Priss pressed her head into Liam's palm then rolled over and stretched her legs out, giving him free access to her back.

Chuckling, he petted her with more confidence now, stroking her thick fur in slow sweeps. "So we're friends now, hmm? Maybe you decided to cut me some slack on account of how fond you are of Mallory and Oliver." He grinned. "If so, I'll take it."

And he could understand. He'd grown more than fond of Mallory and Oliver over the past months. He continued petting the cat, his smile growing even more.

After a few moments, his cell phone buzzed in his back pocket and reluctantly, he withdrew his hand and stood. "Sorry, Miss Priss. I need to take this."

He pulled the cell phone from his back pocket and answered, grinning as Miss Priss stood, stretched then sashayed away.

"Liam?"

The urgency in Mallory's voice made him freeze. "What is it? Is something wrong with Oliver?"

"No. It's…it's Gayle."

His legs were already moving, carrying him swiftly out of the stable and across the grounds. "What do you mean? What's happened?"

Mallory didn't answer right away—her silence more than telling—and he walked faster. The whole sky had turned pink, the rosy light reflecting off the white siding of the main house, casting a strong glow across the front lawn. A chorus of toads and crickets swelled in the distance, blending with the panicked buzz in his ears.

"Just come quick, okay?" Mallory said, her voice strained. "Please hurry."

He disconnected the call, shoved the cell phone in his back pocket and ran. He took the stairs two at a time, moving as quickly as he could to the second story of the main house. Mallory was standing outside Gayle's room. Her lips quivered and her face was streaked with tears.

He stumbled and drew to a stop, his chest burning. "What is it?"

"She won't wake up," Mallory whispered. "I've tried CPR but... I think she—"

Liam, his heart pounding, walked past her, entered the room and sat on the edge of the bed beside where his mother lay.

"Mom?"

Her eyes remained closed and her chest still.

He touched her hand. It was cold. There was no pulse.

"Mom?" It was barely a whisper that didn't require an answer. He knew she was gone.

"I called an ambulance," Mallory said from near his shoulder. "They should be here soon."

Liam looked up, his eyes meeting hers. "At least she's at peace now."

"Oh, Liam," she whispered.

He faced his mother again and moments later, Mallory's hands settled on his shoulders and her temple pressed gently against his. They stayed that way for several minutes until the first responders arrived.

Liam went through the motions, keeping out of the way as the paramedics worked, accepting the news of his mother's death stoically and without surprise, then stepped aside as the first responders carried Gayle away.

The sun had set by the time the ambulance left. Liam watched it disappear around a curve as he stood on the front porch, then his knees seemed to buckle, and he sagged onto the top step and lowered his face in his hands. Heavy sobs wracked his body, and he covered his face, hiding the tears.

"Liam?"

Mallory sat beside him on the step, wrapped her arms around him and hugged him close, swaying gently from side to side. Her soft hands smoothed his hair from his brow, wiped the tears from his cheeks and held him close as he continued to cry. He buried his face against her neck, absorbing her warmth and strength, finding some comfort there.

He stayed in her arms for over an hour, allowing his tears to flow freely as Mallory held him and continued rocking gently from side to side. He felt wrung out now, all the tears having left him, embarrassment taking their place.

"I'm sorry," he rasped, lifting his head from her chest and easing away.

Mallory cupped his face and urged him to meet her eyes. "You have nothing to be sorry for, Liam."

"You loved her, too," he whispered, watching a tear roll down her cheek.

"Yes," she whispered brokenly. A second tear followed the first. "I loved her very much."

The pain in her eyes reflected his own. He lowered his head and brushed his lips across her forehead, trying his best to thank her without being able to say the words. When her eyes fluttered shut, he kissed the corners of her eyes, too, then drifted his thumbs over her cheeks, gathering her tears against his skin as she'd done for him.

On the step nearby, the baby monitor crackled and Oliver's cry emerged.

"I need to go to him," she whispered, pressing her cheek against his palm.

Liam nodded and released her. "Do you mind if I come?"

She stood and reached out, taking his hand in hers, and tugged him to his feet. They walked silently up the stairs, hand in hand, into the nursery. Oliver was crying louder now, his demanding wails filling the room.

Mallory walked to the crib, lifted Oliver in her arms and whispered soothing words as she carried him to the changing table. Liam stood close by as she changed Oliver's diaper, dressed him in a fresh onesie and lifted him into her arms again.

"Would you like to hold him for a while?" she asked.

Liam nodded and sat in the rocking chair, holding out his arms as Mallory settled Oliver against his chest. Oliver looked up at him, his heavy eyelids beginning to close and a sleepy smile crossing his face.

Liam sat there for a while, cradling Oliver in his arms and rocking gently back and forth in the same way Mallory had with him. Soon, Oliver had drifted off again, his pink lips parting and his soft breaths coming rhythmically.

The sight of Oliver, happy and healthy, breathing deep and even, soothed the pain in his heart.

What a blessing this was. To be surrounded by two people he loved after losing someone so dear. The thought evoked a fresh surge of tears and he blinked rapidly, drifting the back of his knuckles gently over Oliver's cheek.

"I love you, Oliver," he whispered softly. He looked up, met Mallory's eyes across the room and said the words his heart shouted loud and clear. "I love you both."

Liam said he loved us, Oliver.

It happened just a few minutes ago when he was holding you. Just as simple and surprising as that.

Mallory looked up from the notepad, shifted to a more comfortable position on the edge of her bed then continued writing.

We lost Gayle today. She had a great time playing with you outside earlier this afternoon, then she lay down for a nap and—

She wiped a tear from her cheek.

But she remembered Liam. She spoke of him today while she was holding you. She said all the things that I've noticed about him that are great. She said she hoped you'd grow up to be like him.

That made Liam happy. You should've seen his face. It's hurt him so much to think that Gayle had no memory left of him but even though she didn't recognize him, she spoke of him. What a blessing for God to give Liam before Gayle had to go away.

Mallory closed her eyes and swallowed hard, silencing a sob. She glanced over her shoulder and looked across the hall, catching a glimpse of Liam as he continued rocking in the chair as he held Oliver in the nursery.

You're still with him now as I write this. Liam started crying again and I thought it best to give him some space and privacy. I left him alone with you for a while. He's been through so much today and I know you make him happy.

You're such a comfort to him. I could tell the moment I put you in his arms that you eased his pain. He's always wanted a son, I think. He loves you so much, Oliver. So very, very much.

And I love him, too.

Mallory bit her lip and looked out the window. There

were no stars out tonight. Instead, clouds had rolled in, covering the moon, and it was darker than ever outside.

He loves you, Oliver. I have no doubts about that. But I wonder, if you weren't mine...if it were just me that had come to Pine Creek Farm, would he still feel the same?

I know Liam loves you, Oliver.

But would he still love me if I didn't have you?

Chapter Ten

By the next afternoon, Liam's brother, Holt, and Jessie arrived at Pine Creek Farm with their three children. Liam and Holt hugged immediately when Holt and his family entered the main house, then the two men walked up the stairs to Gayle's room and shut the door, grieving together in private, sharing memories of their mother and discussing logistics of the funeral, visitation and reception for friends and family that would occur at Pine Creek Farm over the coming days.

Downstairs, Mallory and Jessie spent some time together with the children in the living room, consoling them in the loss of their grandmother and leaning on each other for support in dealing with their own grief. When the children's tears had stopped, Mallory and Jessie prepared a light lunch, chatting as they worked to catch up on each other's activities over the past few months while Jessie and Holt's twin boys, Cody and Devin, entertained their younger sister, Ava.

Before long, Liam and Holt returned downstairs and joined everyone for lunch in the dining room. The meal was a silent affair, everyone doing their best to carry on in the absence of Gayle, but an empty chair that remained at the dining table was a constant reminder of how much they'd lost.

After eating, Holt's twin boys became antsy and in need of a distraction. Liam, his eyes heavy and shadowed, suggested that he and Holt take the boys down to the pond to fish for a couple of hours.

"Are you sure you're up for that?" Mallory asked as he led the two boys toward the front door.

He paused and glanced over his shoulder at her, trying to smile but it was halfhearted at best. "It'll do us all good, I think," he said. "The sunshine and fresh air will help."

That, at least, Mallory could agree with.

Last night, after Liam had finished rocking Oliver back to sleep in the nursery, Mallory had tucked Oliver in his crib, kissed him good night then walked with Liam out into the hallway. Liam was no longer crying but he looked exhausted, and he'd watched her expectantly, studying her face silently, waiting for her to speak.

When she had remained silent and began fidgeting awkwardly with the hem of her shorts as they stood on the landing, he had said good-night and went downstairs to his room.

Mallory had stood there long after he'd left, knowing what he was hoping to hear from her, and disappointed with herself for not having the courage to say it.

She loved him—she had no doubts about the intensity of her feelings for him. Her doubts lay elsewhere.

"They'll be fine," Jessie said as the front door closed behind Liam, Holt and the boys. "Besides, with them gone and now that Ava's down for her nap, I'll have a chance to get to know Oliver a little better."

With that, Jessie stood and walked around the dining room table to where Oliver lay in his bassinet. Smiling, she gathered Oliver in her arms then returned to her seat at the table and cradled him close.

"He's so beautiful, Mallory."

"Thank you," she whispered.

Mallory smiled as Jessie combed her fingers lovingly through Oliver's dark hair, then walked over to the window. She looked out at the front lawn, watching as Holt and Liam, the twin boys between them, walked across the grounds toward a small shed near the stable.

More than likely, Liam kept rods and tackle there. They would probably gather up fishing poles and bait then stroll back to the pond for an afternoon of fishing. Standing there, eyeing the two men from a distance, she had difficulty discerning the difference between Liam's and Holt's tall, muscular frames. They were so similar in stature and both reached out occasionally to ruffle one of the boy's hair affectionately.

"Jessie?" Mallory asked.

"Hmm?"

"Can I ask you something personal?"

"After all the questions I asked you when we first met at Hummingbird Haven?" Jessie glanced over her shoulder and smiled. "Ask away."

Mallory glanced once more at the two men and boys walking across the grounds, then faced Jessie. "How did you know Holt was in love with you?"

Jessie's brows rose. "Well, now, that's definitely a question."

Mallory winced and held up her hand. "I'm sorry, I don't mean to pry, I just—"

Jessie shook her head, looked down at Oliver and grinned. "We don't mind, do we, Oliver?" She looked back up at Mallory and laughed. "Well, I guess I knew when he told me so, for one."

The teasing tone of her voice coaxed a smile from Mallory. "Fair enough. But how else did you know?"

Jessie thought for a moment, then said, "It was the little things mostly. The way he was more concerned with my comfort than his. How he would go out of his way to make me happy and how considerate he was of my thoughts and feelings—especially when it came to the boys." She looked down at Oliver, a wistful expression appearing. "I'm unable to carry children of my own," she said softly.

Mallory frowned and glanced over her shoulder at the twin boys, who walked between Liam and Holt. "But I thought—"

"Cody and Devin are Holt's children and mine," Jessie stated firmly, "but biologically, they only belong to Holt. Holt left Cody and Devin with me at Hummingbird Haven not long after they were born. He wasn't ready to be a father then and I was just grateful to have the chance to be a mom. I wanted to adopt Cody and Devin but Holt came back right around the time I decided to file and told me he wanted to raise them himself."

Jessie shrugged. "We were at an impasse, you see? But I think that was God's way of nudging us together. We worked together to help the boys get to know him and keep them happy and I decided to give them up so Holt would be happy but as it turned out, Holt wasn't happy unless I was in the picture, too. We married, I adopted the boys and we both adopted Ava."

"Oh," Mallory said quietly. "But...say, for instance, that Cody and Devin hadn't been part of the equation. How would you have known that Holt really loved you?"

Jessie stopped rocking Oliver in her arms and shifted

in her chair to face Mallory fully. "What's happened, Mallory? What are you really asking me?"

Sighing, Mallory bit her lip and hesitated. She glanced down at Oliver, who slept peacefully now, then summoned the courage to face Jessie again. "Liam told me he loved me last night."

Silence descended as Jessie absorbed the news. Her mouth opened and closed several times as though she meant to speak but thought better of it.

"Actually, he said he loved us," Mallory said, motioning between herself and Oliver. "Not just me—but *us*."

Understanding dawned on Jessie's face. "And now… you're wondering if Oliver weren't part of the equation, would Liam still love you?"

"Yes," Mallory said, her neck burning.

Jessie sank back in her seat, blew out a heavy breath and cradled Oliver closer. "And this happened last night? After losing Gayle?" At Mallory's nod, she groaned softly and muttered under her breath, "I was afraid of this."

Mallory's frown deepened. "Afraid of what?"

Jessie blushed. "Oh, no—please, I didn't mean it that way. What I meant is, Liam and I had a conversation very similar to what you're suggesting a few months ago."

Mallory shook her head. "What kind of conversation?"

Jessie looked down, her gaze focused on Oliver. "A few days after you first arrived at Pine Creek Farm, I called Liam just to check in on you. To see how things were going. I could tell from the way he spoke that he was happy to have you here at the farm, helping with Gayle." She smiled gently. "And I know from the way Liam spoke about you and Gayle during later conversations, that Gayle truly benefited from you being here. But I can also tell that Liam was getting attached to the idea of you living here with Oliver."

Mallory looked at Oliver. "On a permanent basis, you mean?"

Jessie nodded. "When we spoke that day, he mentioned several things he planned to do in the future, like taking Oliver fishing, for one." She held up a hand. "Not that he'd even met Oliver at that time." She laughed self-consciously. "I mean, Oliver hadn't even been born then, but Liam was already making plans for having a little boy in his life."

Mallory sagged back against the window, her hands curling around the windowsill. "He was excited at the idea of having a baby around?"

"Yes," Jessie said quietly. "That doesn't mean that he only wanted the baby though. It's just…well, Liam has lived here at Pine Creek Farm his entire life. Holt has had a chance to travel, to tour the rodeo circuit, experience the world and decide what he really wanted out of life. Holt chose a life at Hummingbird Haven with me, the boys and Ava." She hesitated. "Thing is, I don't think Liam has ever really had that chance. I mean, the chance to really think about what he wants out of life and choose his own path."

"Because he stayed with Gayle after his father left?" Mallory asked.

"In part," Jessie said. "But he also has another reason that may be influencing how he feels about you and Oliver. He had known Gayle was getting worse for quite some time now. He and Holt didn't speak of the possibility of her passing often, but they did on occasion. Liam knew he would lose Gayle at some point, and I think he wondered at times what would come next for him."

Mallory closed her eyes, her stomach sinking as she shook her head slowly. "And there I came, knocking on your door the night he stayed at Hummingbird Haven."

"Mallory, please don't misunderstand me. I don't mean

to say with any certainty that that's the case. It's just that…" She grimaced. "Well, I care about you and Oliver, too— very much. And I know from experience that it's easy to get attached when you're helping others, like Liam has helped you. The last thing I'd want in the world is for you to be hurt or disappointed again. You asked me what I thought and I'm trying to be honest and open with my answer."

Mallory opened her eyes and looked at Jessie. "And that's what I wanted. I wanted your honest opinion and I'm grateful you gave it to me."

Jessie bit her lip, her gaze moving from Mallory to Oliver and back. "I don't know that I have the answers you're looking for and I don't want you to just blindly accept my advice. I'd feel so much better if you spoke to Liam about this."

Mallory glanced over her shoulder and looked out the window. Liam, Holt and the boys were out of sight now. "I know what he'll say if I ask." She looked at Jessie again. "The problem is, I just won't know if he truly means it. And then I'll be right back where I started."

Jessie was quiet for a moment then asked, "Do you love him?"

"Yes," Mallory whispered. "I love him very much."

"Then maybe…"

As Jessie continued to hesitate, Mallory pushed away from the window, straightened and gestured that she continue. "Please. Tell me. I'd really like to hear what you think."

Jessie sighed. "If you love Liam, maybe give him—and yourself—some time and space so that you can both reflect on what it is you each really want now that Gayle is gone."

Mallory rubbed her temples. An ache had formed there. It began to spread down the back of her neck at the thought of doing what Jessie suggested. "I need to leave Pine Creek Farm anyway," she whispered. "With Gayle gone, it's best that Oliver and I have a place of our own rather than live with Liam as we are now. I could find a place for Oliver and me temporarily until I decide on something permanent. Maybe check with one of the women in the ladies' group at the church I attend with Liam. That way, Liam will have the house to himself and can decide how he truly feels without our influence."

Jessie nodded slowly. "That might be for the best."

"What I'm afraid of," Mallory said softly, "is that he'll realize that he only loves Oliver. Then he'll change his mind about wanting me in his life."

Jessie smiled confidently, but doubt lingered in her eyes. "If he truly loves you, he won't."

"You change your mind about swapping out that worm for a cricket?"

Liam glanced to his left where Holt stood by his side in front of the pond at Pine Creek Farm. Holt's sons, Cody and Devin, stood on the other side of Holt, holding their fishing rods and watching their corks bob in the rippling water. They'd been fishing for over an hour but none of them had caught any bream yet.

Liam looked at his own fishing line, untouched by fish, which continued to float idly deep in the center of the pond. "I just might change my mind. Can't do any worse than I am right now."

"Why ain't the fish biting, Uncle Liam?" Cody asked, frowning up at him from where he stood on the bank.

His nephew's disappointed pout made Liam smile. "It's the wrong time of day, I suppose." He tilted his head back and squinted up at the sky. "It's pretty hot out in the afternoon. Those fish are probably snuggled deep in that water, cooling off and taking a nap."

"So, when's the best time to try to catch them?" Devin asked, reeling in his line.

"Bright and early—first thing in the morning, dude." Holt reached down and ruffled Devin's hair.

"So, can we come out tomorrow morning?" Cody asked. "First thing? Bright and early, like you said?"

Holt shook his head. "I'm afraid not. Your grandmother's funeral is tomorrow and we'll be tied up with that most of the day."

The boys' shoulders slumped and they both faced the pond again, their sad eyes roving over the water.

Liam knelt, bringing himself to eye level with the boys. "Hey. There's a secret spot out here. One where I'll bet you'll get a nibble or two no matter how good the fish are sleeping."

The boys' eyes brightened.

"Where?" Cody asked.

"Show us," Devin said.

Liam pointed at a weeping willow tree on the other side of the pond, its droopy branches dancing lightly over the surface of the water with each push of the summer breeze. "Right there, under that tree. There's a tangle of roots at the base of that tree. Stand right smack-dab in the middle of them, throw your line out and I guarantee you'll get at least one nibble."

Devin yanked his line, reeling it in quickly, looped his hook onto the rod, then took off around the pond, shouting over his shoulder as he ran, "I'm getting the first bite!"

Cody followed suit, reeling in his line and darting after his brother. After a few steps though, he stopped abruptly, turned and ran back to Liam. He threw his arms around

Liam's neck and kissed his cheek. "Thank you for showing us the secret spot, Uncle Liam."

Liam ruffled his hair and smiled. "You're welcome."

Those boys were so adorable, he found himself unable to deny them anything most days.

Cody took off again, joining his brother, and the two boys ran around the pond and set up below the weeping willow tree, casting their lines in and laughing as the corks bobbed in the water.

"Takes you back, doesn't it?" Holt asked quietly by his side.

Liam stood, reeled in his line and cast it out again. "That it does."

Cody and Devin were the spitting image of Holt. They reminded Liam of himself and Holt when they had been the same age, fishing together under the weeping willow, laughing and chatting, looking for some new trouble to get into on the farm. He and his brother had been inseparable at that age.

"Those were some of the best days of my life," Liam said. "When we were kids, the whole world was a playground. We could run at full speed for hours, without stopping."

Holt chuckled. "I'd like to see you try that now."

Liam raised one eyebrow. "I'd watch that, if I were you. I may be a few minutes older than you, but we're basically the same age."

They exchanged wry glances and laughed once more, but their laughter faded when the reason for their recent reunion returned fresh in their minds.

"I wish I'd known you were going to the funeral home this morning," Holt said. "I would've made sure to leave Hummingbird Haven a lot earlier so that I could go with you and help you with planning the funeral for tomorrow."

Liam shrugged. "It was mostly already handled. Mom took care of things ahead of time." He sighed. "She was so afraid of leaving things behind that were unsettled and didn't want to cause me any extra work."

Holt nodded. "She always took care of us." He glanced at Liam and smiled. "And you took great care of her at the end, Liam. Thank you for that."

Liam stood there silently, reeling his line in a few inches, allowing his mind to rove over the past few months. "It wasn't only my doing," he said quietly. "Mallory was closer to Mom than just about anyone by the end."

"Jessie's been telling me over the past few months how big of a help you said Mallory's been for Mom."

"Yeah," Liam said. "She's been a lot more than a help."

They fell silent again, reeling in their lines and tossing them out twice to new spots in the pond.

Liam listened to the water lap against the grassy bank, thoughts tangling in his mind and intense emotions swirling in his heart. "I'm going to ask Mallory to marry me."

"Don't."

Holt's response was as blunt as Liam's statement.

Liam jerked in surprise, his brother's one-word admonishment making him bristle. "What do you mean, *don't*?"

Holt looked at him then, his hazel eyes—the exact same shade as his own—peering deeply into his. "You're in the midst of grieving, Liam. And so is Mallory. From what you and Jessie have told me, Mallory loved Mom just as much as we did, so she's gotta be hurting pretty hard right now."

"I know that," Liam said. "But that's all the more reason to—"

"No, it's not," Holt said firmly. "This is the worst possible time for you to propose right now. With Mom gone, her routine has changed and your whole life has changed.

This isn't the best time to make a major decision—or commitment—like that."

"It didn't come to me overnight, if that's what you're assuming," Liam said sharply, facing the water again. "I've been thinking about it for quite some time."

"How much time?"

Liam shrugged.

"A few months, maybe?" Holt asked quietly. "Or just days after she got here?" When Liam didn't respond, he added, "Jessie told me that you and she had a talk a few months ago, not long after Mallory came to the farm and started taking care of Mom."

Liam tensed, his eyes closing slowly as he reflected upon the content of that uncomfortable conversation.

"She said you were already talking about spending time with Oliver," Holt said. "Already making plans for showing him around the farm when he was older and fishing in this pond like we are now." Holt sighed. "I'm not suggesting that you not ever ask Mallory to marry you—she's a wonderful woman and I'd be over the moon for you. All I'm asking is that you just take some more time. Time to adjust to what your life will be like now without Mom around. You can finally take the time to rest and do whatever you feel like doing without obligation or expectations."

Liam dragged his hand over his face. "I don't understand why you and Jessie are so hung up on me doing something different or leaving the farm and—"

"That's not it," Holt said. "Not it at all. We're just very aware of the fact that you've sacrificed a lot of years to take care of Mom and her childhood home. I can't tell you how much I still regret—" His voice breaking, Holt turned his head and looked away, staring across the grounds. After a moment, he faced Liam again. "Some days I wish

I would've stayed with you and Mom after Dad left. If I'd stayed, you would've had more freedom then. You would've been able to travel or go to college or choose whatever you wanted to do in life. As things stood, after Dad left then I left, too, you were stuck with everything on your shoulders."

"I wasn't stuck," Liam said firmly. "I chose to be here."

"I don't mean to imply that you would've chosen to leave if I hadn't. I just regret not helping you as much as I should have." Holt tugged his line in, aimed for a new spot in the pond then tossed it out again. "I won't say that I regret the way my life's turned out though. And if I had the choice, I can't say that I'd go back and do things differently because if I did, I may have never met Jessie or had the boys."

Liam looked at the twins again. Cody was pointing at Devin's cork. They both jumped with excitement and leaned forward, staring at Devin's cork as it bobbed in the water.

"Devin got a bite, Dad!" Cody shouted across the pond.

Holt smiled and waved then called out, "Nice job, dude! Now keep your eyes on it and snatch the line in when the fish bites again."

The boys returned their attention to the cork, remaining motionless as they stared into the water.

Liam chuckled. "You got two fantastic boys right there." He smiled at Holt. "And you're a fantastic dad."

"You will be, too, one day," Holt said softly as he faced him again. "Or is that why you're so anxious to ask Mallory to marry you? Are you looking to be Oliver's dad right now?"

"I love Oliver," Liam said. "Any man would be lucky to be his dad. But that's not the reason. I love Mallory, too."

"But do you think she's ready for another husband?" Holt peered at him. "She accepted your job offer and came out here to start over and make a new life for herself and her baby. Are you sure settling down permanently in the first place she moved to, and remarrying after what she went through with her ex-husband is what she really wants to do?"

Liam gazed across the pond again. A hollow formed in his gut. "I… I haven't thought about it in that way."

"You're a good man," Holt said, "and I'd be shocked if Mallory didn't love you back. But this is her chance, Liam. This is Mallory's chance to start fresh and make a new life for herself. One where she's safe and in control of her own life. You know her better than me," he said softly, "but I wonder, if you ask her to marry you so soon after you've met, considering the circumstances, if you might not scare her away?"

Liam's throat tightened as he watched the boys whoop and holler, pulling hard on the fishing rods, reeling in a bream.

"All I'm saying is," Holt whispered, "don't propose yet. Not right now. Give it time until you—and Mallory—are certain it's what you both want and not just a result of circumstances."

Liam didn't respond—he couldn't. His throat had tightened and his mind reeled. He'd told Mallory he loved her, but she hadn't said it back. And now Holt was bringing a new doubt into his mind. In the beginning, he'd wanted to help Mallory out of kindness, sure. But now things were different. *He* felt differently and he hoped she did, too.

But considering all she'd been through and if what Holt said was true, Mallory may not want to marry again. Not now, or possibly ever. And the thought of losing Mallory and Oliver—especially so soon after losing Gayle—was too painful to bear.

Chapter Eleven

The next day, Gayle's funeral went as planned. The pews of the church were full of friends and family who mourned her passing. The sermon was beautiful and Liam, sitting beside Mallory and holding Oliver in his arms throughout the service, was able to hold back the tears that brimmed on his lower lashes each time he looked down at Oliver's smile.

It was a difficult day that Mallory knew Liam was anxious to put behind him.

After they left the church and returned to Pine Creek Farm, Mallory carried Oliver inside the main house, settled him in his bassinet in the kitchen and began pulling casseroles, ham and desserts that friends and family had dropped off out of the freezer and refrigerator and began warming them up.

"Here," Jessie said, striding into the kitchen and dropping her purse on the dining table. "Let me help you with that."

They fell into an easy rhythm, working fast and efficiently, laying out the food on the dining table, filling glass after glass with sweet tea and directing those who dropped in to pay their respects to Liam and the rest of the family to the refreshments. In between, they gathered up dirty paper plates and cups and tossed them in trash bags and loaded the dishwasher with used silverware.

Dozens of neighbors and friends continued to pour in, studying the pictures of Gayle that Liam had set out the night before and offering their condolences to Liam. Mallory thought he held up well through it all, remaining patient and polite through the deluge of visitors. He'd even laughed once or twice at something someone had said.

Despite everything going as planned, the day had been long and by the time the last round of guests had arrived, it seemed even longer.

"Why don't you take Oliver up to the nursery?" Jessie asked, taking the dirty plates Mallory carried out of her hands and putting them in the sink. "I can handle the rest of this on my own."

"But—"

"You've done enough," Jessie said firmly. "You've been at it all day and you look like you could tip over at any minute." She hugged her then smiled. "Go ahead. Go sit down with Oliver and put your feet up for a while."

Too tired to argue, Mallory complied. She picked up Oliver from his bassinet and carried him through the kitchen and into the hallway.

"Mallory." Liam walked out of the living room and joined her at the foot of the stairs. "Are you putting him down for a nap?"

She nodded. "He's worn out."

"I know the feeling," he said quietly. He lifted his hand and drifted the back of one finger down her cheek. "I think you do, too. You look exhausted."

Despite the circumstances, Mallory found herself smiling. "What a charmer you are."

He had the good grace to blush. "You know what I mean. You're always beautiful, Mallory."

Her smile faded and she looked down, watching as Oliver frowned and began kicking against her arms.

"Hey there," Liam said, gently lifting one of Oliver's hands in his. "You giving your mama a hard time? She's been taking care of everyone today, so you should cut her some slack, okay?"

Mallory's smile returned. "You know the feeling, don't you? You're always taking care of everyone else no matter the occasion."

Liam met her gaze, admiration in his eyes. "I can't thank you enough for all you've done the past couple of days. And what you did for Mom." His throat moved on a hard swallow. "I hope you know how much I appreciate all you've done."

"It's the least I could do," she whispered, "considering all you've done for us. Oliver and I owe you more than we could ever repay."

Liam frowned as he studied her expression. "Mallory—"

"I should put him down," she said, lifting her chin toward Oliver. "Before he starts testing out his lungs again."

Liam nodded then stepped back so she could climb the stairs to the second floor to the nursery. Voices from downstairs, slightly muffled, could still be heard on the upper landing. She shut the door behind her and the nursery closed around them like a soft cocoon, peaceful and quiet. She carried Oliver over to the rocking chair and sat down.

The day had taken its toll on Oliver, too. His eyes were heavy but he was fussy and unable to relax.

"I know, sweet boy," Mallory whispered, lifting him up to her shoulder and rubbing slow, gentle circles over his back. "We both have a lot on our minds, don't we?"

She'd barely slept last night, the conversation she'd had with Jessie about Liam yesterday still weighing heavy on her mind.

Right now she had a reprieve from the difficult conversation she knew she'd have to have with Liam, considering the house was full of family and guests. But once Holt, Jessie, their kids and all the rest of the family and friends left, she'd be on her own again with Liam. There'd be no way around it then. She'd have to have a conversation with him. They would have to discuss the future and her place in it.

The problem was, she was afraid. She was afraid of losing Liam and having to leave Pine Creek Farm.

But there were no other options, really. She needed to do as Jessie had suggested. She'd have to come right out and ask Liam how he felt about her. If he loved her—even without Oliver. And even then, if he answered the way she wanted him to and hoped he would, she wouldn't be sure if he truly meant it.

Because it's the right thing to do.

That's what he had said once. And that was who Liam was—a good man who could be trusted and depended upon. He would do the right thing in any situation, even if it cost him.

And doing the right thing in this situation wouldn't be enough. Not for her and not for Oliver.

"Oh, Oliver," she whispered. "How can we ever leave this place? How can we ever leave Liam?"

Oliver had grown quiet, his soft breaths coming deep and even between parted lips.

Sighing, she stood, carried Oliver across the room and placed him in his crib. He rolled his head to the side, pressed his cheek against the soft mattress and pulled his knees under his belly.

Mallory smiled. He looked so peaceful now, so at ease. She wished she could feel the same.

Two days later, when Holt, Jessie and their children said their goodbyes, climbed into Holt's truck and drove down the long driveway of Pine Creek Farm, Liam stood in the front yard and held Oliver in his arms then, too. He knew his brother and Jessie had work to get back to at Hummingbird Haven but he hated to see them leave all the same. Over the past few days, he'd grown accustomed to having his family with him, all of the guest rooms in the main house full and the dining table surrounded by the faces of loved ones at every meal.

It would be a long stretch before he saw his brother again. More than likely, the Thanksgiving holidays would be their next gathering.

He waved goodbye again, knowing the boys would be looking back at him from the rear window of the cab until the truck turned onto the highway and disappeared.

Oliver, feeling neglected, wiggled in Liam's arms, his bare feet kicking his elbow.

"He's getting fussy," Mallory said from where she stood by his side on the front lawn. "I think it's time to put him down for the night."

Liam drifted his finger over Oliver's soft cheek, watching as Oliver's eyelids closed slowly. "Yeah," he said. "I think you're right. He's had a busy few days with a lot of attention from a lot of new people."

Mallory walked with him as he carried Oliver up the front porch steps, into the main house then climbed the stairs into the nursery.

"He's been worn out with all the commotion lately," Mallory said, smiling as Liam settled Oliver in his crib.

And so was she.

Liam studied her face as she bent over the crib and drifted a kiss across Oliver's forehead. Mallory had borne the brunt of the workload over the past few days as they'd attended the funeral, prepared the house to receive friends and family afterward and continued to receive drop-in guests who brought various casseroles and side dishes for the family.

Mallory had truly been a blessing. She'd gone out of her way to take care of everything, refusing to allow Liam to do anything but focus on healing and spending time with his brother, nephews and niece. But yesterday, he'd reminded her that he would be returning to the normal routine as soon as Holt and Jessie left. Staying busy was the best way to comfort a broken heart and there was plenty to do at Pine Creek Farm.

"You might want to lie down, too," Liam said softly. "You've had a longer day than any of us have."

She'd risen early this morning and cooked breakfast for everyone, having set the table with place settings and plates almost overflowing with scrambled eggs, bacon and waffles prior to Liam waking and joining her in the kitchen. She'd cleaned the entire house afterward, too, changing the bedsheets and towels in every guest room, washing laundry, and sweeping and mopping the floors. Every time he'd offered to help, she'd shooed him away, encouraging him to spend time with his brother, Jessie, the kids and Oliver in peace.

"I think you're right. I could use a nap," she said now, tucking a strand of her long, wavy hair behind her ear. Her hand trembled. "But there's something I'd like to talk with you about first."

Liam smiled, but his stomach churned. "That sounds pretty serious."

Her cheeks reddened. "It is." She walked toward the door. "Do you mind joining me on the front porch? The sun's starting to set and it's cooler now."

Liam nodded and followed her out of the nursery and down the stairs. He sat in a rocking chair beside her on the front porch and they rocked silently for a few minutes, gazing out at the grounds, watching the hot summer sun dip below the horizon.

"You know I can't stay," Mallory said softly.

He continued rocking by her side, staring straight ahead in the same direction that she did. "Even without—" He cleared his throat. "There's still plenty of work available around the farm even without the caretaking position. Maintaining the guest rooms and guesthouses alone is a full-time—"

"I don't mean that," she said. "With Gayle gone, it's not like it was. We're not a married couple and it wouldn't be appropriate. Especially now with Oliver here."

"I could reserve a guest house for you. You and Oliver could stay there, apart from the main house."

"I appreciate the offer, but that wouldn't really resolve the issue."

He frowned. "Then what is the issue?"

She stared back at him silently, then faced the setting sun again. "When you were Cody's and Devin's age or maybe when you were a teenager, what were your dreams for the future?"

Frowning deeper, he looked at the grounds again, too. "I don't know what that has to do with—"

"It has everything to do with it," she said. "Please tell me. I want to know."

He continued rocking, roving his eyes over the landscape, watching as the sky changed colors, turning from blue to gold, pink then red before finally giving way to a starry night sky.

"You don't know, do you?" she asked quietly. There was a rustle of movement by his side and he turned his head to find her looking at him again. "You've never really had the opportunity to choose what you want out of life, have you?"

A wry smile curved his lips. "You've been talking to Jessie and Holt, haven't you?"

"Maybe. But that's not why I asked."

"I don't know what you want me to say, Mallory."

"I want you to tell me what you want." A plea entered her eyes. "I want you to tell me that there's something that you've dreamed of having. That you've thought about what it'd be like after your mom was gone. That instead of taking care of others and always sacrificing for someone else, that there's something you really want of your own."

Oh, he wanted. He wanted so much.

He wanted to marry Mallory. He wanted to be a father to Oliver. He wanted the three of them to be a family. He wanted to fill the main house with more children and one day, hopefully, grandchildren. He wanted—

Don't.

Liam shot to his feet at the memory of Holt's voice. He walked over to the porch rail, leaned onto his hands and ducked his head. "I know what I want," Liam rasped.

"Please tell me."

"I want to marry you." He spoke before thinking better of it, then spun around, his breath coming in short, shallow bursts. "I want to be a father to Oliver. I want you and Oliver to be under this roof with me every day, every night, every morning. I want you to let me love you and Oliver with everything I've got because I can't imagine the future without you and him. I want to be there for you and Oliver for as long as I can, in every way."

His answer seemed to disappoint her.

She looked down at her hands, wringing them together in her lap, her eyes sad. "Why?" she asked quietly. "Because it's the right thing to do?"

"Mallory—"

"You told me yourself that that was why you offered me a job and decided to help me." She smiled, but there were tears in her eyes. "You're a good man, Liam. The best I've ever known. But I don't want to be a cause of charity for you. I don't want you to marry me out of loneliness and then regret your commitment later. And I don't want you to realize, when it's too late, that had circumstances been different, had we not met as we did, that you'd be making a very different decision right now as far as what to do with your future."

Liam lifted his hand in appeal. "I love you and Oliver."

Her chin wobbled and she closed her eyes briefly before meeting his gaze head-on again. "I know you love Oliver. But do you love me? Do you truly love me? Or are you just in love with the idea of having a wife and child?"

Her words caught him off guard. They evoked an unexpected surge of emotions—hurt, frustration, anger and... doubt.

"You realize," she said softly, "that everything you've said you wanted—every time you've said you love me—you've said it in terms of me and Oliver."

He remained silent, his heart pounding in his chest as he wracked his mind, reviewing his words, searching himself to see if there was any truth to her assumption.

"If we hadn't met as we did," she said, "and if it wasn't

Oliver and me—if it was just me—would you still feel the same?"

If it was...just her? He hesitated, searching for the right words, but not finding them. Oliver was rooted in his heart as deeply as she was. It'd be impossible to imagine he didn't exist, and he had no desire to.

"I don't know how to answer you," he said quietly. "I don't know what you want me to say and I don't know that there is anything that I could say that would make you understand how I truly feel. To make you believe me."

Mallory stood and moved closer, her hand lifting as if to touch his face before lowering back to her side without making contact. "I just wanted to be sure that you believed it," she said quietly. "And I think I have my answer."

She stepped away and he moved to speak but—

"I want to be sure that having me in your life is what you really want and not a result of circumstances," she said. "And I need some time to do the same for myself. I need time to stand on my own feet with Oliver, move forward independently and do everything I can to ensure that neither one of us is choosing this out of loneliness or fear. I owe that to Oliver, at the very least."

He closed his eyes, wincing as a surge of pain streaked through him. She would leave now and take Oliver with her. And he had to let her go. It was the only hope he had of getting her to understand. To help her see what he already saw and know in her own heart what he already knew in his.

"For how long?" he asked.

She bit her lip. "I don't know. Long enough for both of us to heal and know how we truly feel."

He rubbed his forehead and sighed. "Where will you go?"

"I spoke with Pam yesterday and she offered me a room

at her place until I'm able to find an apartment. I'll pack tonight and ask her to pick me and Oliver up tomorrow."

Liam nodded, his thoughts tangled and his heart aching. "I'll help you pack."

What else could he do?

The next morning, Liam loaded Oliver's crib into the bed of his truck, tied it down securely and watched as Pam loaded the last of Mallory's bags into the trunk of her car that was parked in front of his truck.

"I think that's everything," Pam said, closing the trunk of her car. She rubbed her hands together briskly and faced Liam. "Mallory's getting Oliver into his car seat now and should be out shortly."

Liam nodded, shoved his hands into his pockets and leaned against the front bumper of his truck. "When you're ready to leave, I'll follow y'all into town, carry Oliver's crib into your house and help unload the rest of the bags."

"Thank you," Pam said, smiling. "That's very kind of you."

Kind. Such a benign word. But for some reason, in that moment and after a night of tossing and turning to memories of Mallory's questions, it felt like an insult.

Though he couldn't blame Mallory for wondering if his feelings for her were genuine. He had, after all, invited her to Pine Creek Farm as a kind, helpful gesture. At the time, he hadn't expected to fall in love with her. And apparently, she was still under the impression that he felt responsible for her somehow and that his love for her stemmed from the fact that she was Oliver's mother.

But there was no truth to that. Unable to sleep, he'd left his bed last night, dressed and walked outside to the firepit. He'd stared up at the stars and had caught himself turning to the empty chair beside him, expecting to see Mallory's face, only to be reminded of the painful fact that she may never join him there again.

He turned away and stared across the field, where one of the hands led several guests astride horses across the grounds in a trail ride.

Pam's hand touched his forearm, her voice gentle. "I know this is hard for you, Liam. And I'm so sorry about Gayle. Please believe me when I say that Mallory is doing this for you just as much—if not more so—than for herself and Oliver."

Liam faced her again and managed to smile. "I don't mean to be difficult or sound put out. It's just a lot of change all at one time."

Pam squeezed his forearm. "I believe that's why Mallory is giving you both some space," she said. "She wants to see you happy just like the rest of us do."

Liam nodded but remained silent. What would make him happy would be to hear Mallory say she loved him. But, it seemed, he'd have to settle on waiting—and hoping—to hear that in time.

And if, after all she'd endured in her previous marriage, she needed time to feel comfortable entering a relationship with him, he'd give her as much as she needed.

The front door opened and Mallory emerged from the house, carrying Oliver, who she'd strapped into the car seat, to Pam's car.

Liam pulled his hands from his pockets and walked over to her. "Would you like some help?"

There were dark circles under her eyes, as though she'd struggled to sleep, too, but she issued a small smile. "Yes, please. Thank you."

Liam took his time installing Oliver's car seat in the

back seat of Pam's car. He lingered for a moment, letting Oliver capture one of his fingers in his tiny palm, his heart breaking just a little more when Oliver cooed and smiled up at him.

"I'm afraid we have to say goodbye for now," Liam whispered. He leaned farther across the back seat, kissed the soft curls on top of Oliver's head then eased away. "I'll see you again soon, little man."

Or, at least, he hoped so.

Mallory and Pam got into Pam's car and Liam returned to his truck, cranked the engine and followed them into town to Pam's house. When they arrived, he unloaded Oliver's crib and carried it inside, then brought in the majority of the bags Mallory had brought, trying to set everything up in the guest room similar to the way it had been in the nursery at Pine Creek Farm.

"I think that's all of it," Mallory said, walking into the room, cradling Oliver in her arms. "Thank you for helping me move, Liam."

He studied her face, stealing a few extra moments to memorize her features. "You're welcome." He hesitated, then shoved his hands into his pockets again and headed for the door. "I'll leave so you and Oliver can get settled in."

"Liam?" Mallory curled her hand over the crook of his elbow and looked up at him, her brown eyes dark with concern. "You're welcome to see Oliver whenever you'd like. Any time, I mean it. Just give me a call and we'll arrange it."

He didn't quite know what to say, and he couldn't say what he wanted. He couldn't tell her he loved her again and beg her to stay. She'd asked for space and he'd given it to her.

"Thank you," he said finally.

"Take care of yourself, Liam."

He bent his head and kissed Oliver's forehead once more then cupped Mallory's cheek in his palm and pressed his lips to her forehead, too, closing his eyes and breathing her in. "And you as well, Mallory."

We left Pine Creek Farm today, Oliver.

You're asleep now in your crib, in a guest room in Pam's house. You went out like a light. You didn't fuss or cry. You settled right in.

I'm pleased your routine wasn't disrupted and that you feel comfortable in Pam's house, but the fact that you took to the change so easily scares me.

Mallory, seated on the edge of the bed in one of Pam's guest rooms, stood, set her notepad aside then walked across the room to the window. She pulled back the curtain slightly and looked outside.

She couldn't see the stars here. Not in the city limits of Pine Creek. Though it was a small town, there were streetlights right outside Pam's house, lining the wide suburban road. It was silent here this time of night. There were no toads or crickets singing by the pond, no crackling fire and no whisper of wind over fields.

Mallory returned to the bed, picked up her notepad, sat down and began writing again.

Pam's house is beautiful and comfortable but it's not the same as Pine Creek Farm. It doesn't feel like home to me. And Liam's not here...

She glanced at the hallway, at the open door of the guest room where Oliver slept.

You're still sleeping soundly as though nothing's changed. Is Liam doing the same? Is he continuing his day and

*night as though nothing's changed? I know he misses you,
but does he miss me at all?*

    That's what scares me, Oliver.

    What if, after some time, he doesn't miss me at all?

Chapter Twelve

Three weeks later, Mallory toured a two-bedroom apartment within the city limits of Pine Creek. It was a ground-level apartment, which meant she wouldn't have to carry Oliver's stroller up the stairs on account of there not being an elevator. The living room was small but was large enough for a couch and a TV, and the two bedrooms made up for the lack of space elsewhere by being connected by a large Jack and Jill bathroom.

"There's a refrigerator and microwave in the kitchen," the landlord said, leading the way from the hallway into the kitchen. "But it's not fully stocked with utensils or pans, so you'll want to bring those and your own dishes."

Mallory glanced briefly about the room. It was clean and large enough to accommodate one person when cooking, which was all Mallory needed and could actually financially afford.

After leaving Pine Creek Farm, she'd stayed home with Oliver for the first week, spending time with him, helping him become familiar with the new surroundings and feel comfortable with Pam. But soon, she'd struck out on her own with Oliver, visiting addresses she'd found on the internet for available apartments and keeping an eye out for any local businesses that might be hiring. But the first order of business had been purchasing a car.

With the money she'd saved from working at Pine Creek Farm and from selling her old car, she had tucked away just enough to afford a small used sedan. It wasn't fancy but it ran smoothly, was dependable and got great gas mileage so she couldn't complain. It was a treat, really, being able to strap Oliver in his car seat, hop in the driver's seat and drive them a few blocks away from Pam's house to sit in the park, enjoy the birds singing and watch other kids play.

Mallory could go anywhere now. Aside from her budgetary considerations, she could live anywhere she wanted, work anywhere she wanted and schedule her days however she wanted.

She was in charge of choosing the decorations for the new home that she and Oliver would occupy. She could hang her clothes in whatever way she pleased or not hang them up at all. She could move about freely in town, not looking over her shoulder all the time, unafraid to meet new people and explore new pursuits.

She finally felt free to live the life she wanted.

Only, no matter how many apartments she toured or how many jobs she investigated as possibilities, her mind—and heart—always kept coming back to Pine Creek Farm. She missed the place she had begun to call home and most of all, she missed Liam.

"—and walking distance from the park," the landlord was saying.

Mallory shook her head. "I'm sorry, I didn't quite catch that."

The landlord, a young blonde woman with pretty green eyes, smiled. "I just said that the park is within walking distance from the apartment." She squatted down, bringing her eyes level with Oliver, who was cradled in Mallory's arms. "I bet you'd like that, wouldn't you? Living right next to a park? When you get a little older, you'll be able to slide down the slides and swing on the swings. You'd enjoy that, wouldn't you?"

Oliver, a bit grumpy on account of it being past his nap time, made a face then buried his nose in Mallory's shirt and cried.

"Oh, goodness," the lady said, standing upright and pressing a hand to her chest. "I didn't mean to upset him."

"You didn't." Mallory smiled. "He hasn't had a nap today, is all. We've been looking at apartments most of the morning and haven't taken a breath yet."

"Well, I hope you'll keep us in mind," she said. "We'd love to have you as new tenants."

Mallory asked a few more questions about the apartment, thanked the landlord for giving her a tour and asked for her card so that she could call if she decided to rent the apartment. Soon after, she took one last look around then left.

Early July was scorching in South Georgia, and she winced as she exited the apartment complex. Humid, sticky air enveloped her as soon as she stepped onto the sidewalk.

Oliver, feeling the heat as well, began to cry again.

"I know," Mallory soothed. "Let's get you in the car and turn on the air conditioner."

By the time she'd driven back to Pam's house, carried Oliver inside and placed him in his crib, he'd already dozed off.

"Oh, but he was tuckered out, wasn't he?" Pam asked, walking in quietly and peering into the crib.

"I kept him out longer than I should have," Mallory whispered. "I just didn't expect it to take so long to tour apartments. Once I started, it made sense to keep going until I reached the end of my list and get it all done in one day."

"Did you find a complex you liked?" Pam asked.

"There was one that's nice enough and within my budget," Mallory said as she fiddled with a teddy bear that she'd tucked into Oliver's crib. "It's right across the street from the park so we could walk there any time we'd like."

"That's good." Pam studied her face. "But you don't really sound too excited."

She wasn't. No matter how hard she tried to stay optimistic about moving into a new apartment, she still couldn't bring herself to stop thinking about Pine Creek Farm... and Liam.

"Well," Mallory said softly, "it's a big step. I want to be sure that wherever we move, Oliver will be happy and safe."

"I completely understand," Pam said, squeezing her hand. "And please keep in mind that you're welcome to stay here as long as you'd like. I love having a baby around the house!" She grinned. "Now, you've had a long day and Oliver's sleeping good, so why don't you join me in the kitchen for a cup of coffee and some fresh-baked chocolate chip cookies?"

Mallory smiled. "It's a bit too hot for coffee for me, but I'll definitely take you up on the cookies."

Pam laughed. "I thought you would. We both have a sweet tooth."

An hour later, they were still sitting in the kitchen, lingering over coffee, lemonade and cookies while Mallory shared the details of the apartments she'd toured earlier that day.

"So, were there any messages left for me while I was gone?" Mallory asked.

Pam scooped a spoonful of sugar into her coffee and stirred. "Don't you really mean to ask if Liam called?"

Mallory sighed. "Am I that transparent?"

"No, not at all." She smiled gently. "You're good at keeping your feelings close to your chest. But you seemed a bit down lately and you're not as enthused about the prospect of a new apartment as I thought you might be."

"I'm not, am I?" Mallory leaned her elbows on the table and propped her chin in her hands. "I just love Pine Creek Farm so much. I miss it so. And Oliver loved it there."

"And you loved living there?" Pam asked.

"Yes."

"And you love Liam, too?"

"Yes."

Mallory stilled, answering Pam's question before she could think better of it.

Pam looked at her face and winced good-naturedly. "I didn't mean to stick my nose into your personal business, but it wasn't hard to tell during the times that I saw you two together that you may have feelings for each other."

Mallory sagged back in her chair and sighed. "I miss him," she whispered.

"I know."

"I just want Liam to be happy," Mallory said. "And I want to do the right thing by Oliver. I just don't know if it's the right time. I mean, Liam and I met under unusual circumstances. I just had Oliver and am trying to be the best mother I can, and we both lost Gayle. I just…it feels like the timing is wrong."

"Oh, Mallory," Pam said softly. "I don't think any of us have any control over that. God tends to do things in His own time and I think it's better to lean on His judgement rather than our own."

Mallory nodded in agreement but remained silent.

"And how do you know that Pine Creek Farm isn't where God wanted you all along?" Pam asked.

Mallory turned over the possibilities in her mind, wondering if meeting Liam, moving to Pine Creek Farm to care for Gayle and falling in love with Liam had been part of God's plan all along. And…if Liam falling in love with her had been part of His plan, too.

The only question was: Was she ready to trust Liam's heart and embrace a new beginning with him?

"I tell you what," Pam said. "You need some time to yourself. Independence Day is tomorrow and Liam always throws a fantastic fireworks display for the guests at Pine Creek Farm. There's free admission and it's open to all residents of Pine Creek without the need of a reservation. Why don't you go? It'll give you a chance to get out of the house, spend some time on your own and see how you feel about returning to the farm…and possibly Liam."

Mallory hesitated. It was tempting, but—

"What about Oliver?" Mallory asked.

"I'll watch him, of course," Pam said, smiling. "I'll take any chance I can get to babysit that sweet child. So do this for me, please. At dusk tomorrow, you hop in that new used car of yours and drive back to Pine Creek Farm. Watch the fireworks, talk to Liam and see how you feel."

Mallory considered this. It would be nice to see Pine Creek Farm again and it'd be wonderful to see Liam. Her heart practically leapt at the thought. "Yes," Mallory said. "That's what I'll do."

The crowd at Pine Creek Farm on July Fourth was a sight to behold.

When Mallory turned onto the long driveway of Pine

Creek Farm the next night, two teenaged boys, holding flashlights, stopped her a few feet down the driveway.

"The back lots are full, ma'am," one of the teens said, leaning on the open window of Mallory's car. "You need to park in this field over here—" he swung his flashlight to the left "—if you want to stay."

Mallory followed the pool of light as it settled on the field behind him. There were two lines of parked trucks and cars and only a few spaces remained.

"Wait a minute," Mallory said, sticking her head out the window and peering through the darkness toward the main house. "You mean to tell me there are so many cars parked near the house that they're backed up all the way out here?"

"Yes, ma'am," he said.

"There are that many people here?" she asked. "I didn't think Pine Creek was that big."

He laughed. "No, ma'am. We get people coming here from all over for the Fourth of July. This isn't even as bad as it gets, from what I'm told. This is my first year working this event, but my friends worked here last year and they told me it was almost twice as bad that year as it is this one."

"Well, that's good," Mallory said, smiling. "Depending on how you look at it. For business, I mean."

Liam, she imagined, was probably very pleased with the turnout. The more exposure Pine Creek Farm received, the more reservations he was likely to book for the guesthouses and trail rides.

"I suppose so." The teen shined his light behind her car then waved his arm. "I'm sorry, but I got someone coming behind you, ma'am. If you don't mind pulling on in and getting parked?"

"Of course," Mallory said, driving the car forward and turning left into the field.

She parked as close as she could to the driveway, cut the engine then got out and walked slowly along the driveway toward the main house. It was almost nine-thirty and the stars were shining brightly. She could see them twinkling between the branches of the magnolia trees that stretched out overhead. She smiled to herself as she thought of the many times she and Gayle had walked the same path, admiring the blooms, chatting, and sometimes strolling in silence, just enjoying the view.

Oh, how she missed Gayle. She knew Liam must miss her, too. She wondered what he'd been doing these weeks that she hadn't seen him. For a while, she'd hoped he would take her up on the offer to see Oliver and had waited impatiently for him to call.

It was ironic, really, that she was longing for him to visit Oliver just so she could see him. She supposed that, in a way, she should take it as a good sign that Liam hadn't pursued seeing Oliver. That, at least, could mean that all the time he'd spent with her and Oliver, he may not have been spending it just to be around Oliver. Perhaps—or at least she hoped—he'd wanted to be in her company just as much, too.

She continued walking, thinking of the many evenings she and Liam had spent sitting beside the firepit behind the main house. Some nights, they sat outside for over two hours, looking at the stars, sometimes sitting in silence, and other times chatting about various things.

She missed that. She missed Liam.

By the time she reached the end of the driveway, the crowd had thickened, and people milled about the grounds, most of them heading around the back of the main house.

Mallory craned her neck, scanning the area for any sign of Liam. He was here somewhere, but it would be almost impossible to find him, given the number of people who'd gathered on the grounds.

"Ten minutes until the show," another teenager, a girl this time, shouted from the edge of the crowd. "Please make your way to the back field, find a comfortable spot and settle in. The show will start soon."

Mallory stepped aside as the rest of the crowd began to move toward the back field. She chose a different path instead, taking a detour through the stable. Not long after she'd entered the stable, she felt a familiar brush of fur at her ankle.

She looked down at Miss Priss, who wound around her legs and meowed. "Well, fancy meeting you here." She bent and scratched the cat's ears, laughing when Miss Priss tilted her head for a better angle. "Oh, you've missed me, huh? Has Liam not been giving you enough attention?"

She petted Miss Priss for another moment or two then walked to the back of the stable and stopped at Sugar's stall. The brown mare sniffed the air then walked over and poked her nose out, snorting softly when Mallory stroked her forehead.

"I've missed you, too," Mallory said. "Have you been taking good care of Liam since I've been gone?"

As if in response, Sugar nudged Mallory's hand, seeking more affection.

Mallory obliged, lingering by Sugar's stall for a few minutes more before the distant pop of firecrackers rang out in the distance.

"Well, I better go," she said, giving Sugar one last pat. "I might miss the whole show if I don't head over there now and snag a good spot."

She left the stable and walked across the field to the back of the main house. Overhead, pops, bangs and whistles continued to ring out, lighting up the sky with dozens of various colors. Mallory stopped near the firepit where several others had gathered, tipped her head back and watched as the fireworks display continued.

Each burst of bright color lit up the fields with dazzling light as it streaked across the sky. Murmurs of appreciation moved through the crowd and Mallory smiled, enjoying the dazzling display.

It went on for a while and Mallory stood still, taking it in, until a hand, big, strong—and familiar—covered hers and squeezed. She turned her head and looked up, finding Liam smiling down at her.

His mouth moved but the pops and bangs overhead drowned out his words, and she pointed to her ear and mouthed, *I can't hear you.*

Laughing, he dipped his head, brought his mouth close to her ear and said, "I'm glad you're here."

His soft breath tickled her earlobe. She smiled and resisted the urge to lift her hand and touch his face. To feel his warm cheek beneath her fingertips.

Dipping his head down again, he said, "This is the best part coming up. Keep your eyes right there."

He pointed at the sky and her gaze followed. Moments later, a new round of fireworks rang out, lighting up the sky with multiple colors that shimmered among the stars.

Laughing with delight, she glanced at Liam. He was still looking up and bright shades of pink, blue, red, white, yellow and purple glowed over his skin. He looked down then and met her eyes, smiling.

She savored the moment, holding his gaze and squeezing his hand just a bit tighter. The moment—surprising and unexpected—was perfect. She'd never felt happier or more hopeful. Standing there, on Pine Creek Farm, with Liam by her side, felt like home just as much as it always had.

Her heart overflowed.

Soon, the fireworks stopped, the lights that had glowed over Liam's skin faded and the crowd sighed with disappointment.

Liam looked down at her with a regretful expression. "I have to go. People will be leaving soon and I need to help direct traffic."

Mallory almost sagged with disappointment. "I should've come sooner."

He stared down at her, his mouth opening and closing as he hesitated, before he finally said, "Come back tomorrow. Or the next day. I'm always here."

Someone called his name and he squeezed her hand once more before releasing it and walking away, calling back over his shoulder, "Come back tomorrow, okay?"

He disappeared into the crowd before she could answer.

She fell in line with the rest of the crowd and walked slowly beneath the magnolias back down the driveway to her car. She lingered for a moment, casting her gaze across the landscape once more, then got in her car and drove away.

I saw Liam today, Oliver.

There was a fireworks display at Pine Creek Farm and it was beautiful. It was the first time in my life that I stood beneath fireworks with someone I loved by my side who loved me in return, the way I deserve.

I miss him, Oliver. I miss working with him, laughing with him and sitting under the stars by his side. My heart knows what it wants. And I hope he knows for sure that he wants the same, too.

This is the last entry I'll write, Oliver. I'm taking a chance I should've taken weeks ago.

I'm hopeful and happy. I'm ready to put the past behind me and move on. I want us to start our new life together and I want Liam to be a part of it, too.

Chapter Thirteen

Two days later, Liam waved at several guests who he'd led on a trail ride as they said their goodbyes, thanked him again and walked away to return to their guest houses at Pine Creek Farm.

"You've had a full day, haven't you, girl?" he asked, patting Sugar on her neck.

Actually, they had both had two full days. For the past forty-eight hours, Liam had done everything he could to keep his mind and hands busy. He'd mucked the stalls both mornings, led extra trail rides to get through the afternoon then washed and groomed the horses before retiring for the night.

It didn't make much difference, though. No matter how hard he worked or how busy he stayed, he still couldn't get Mallory off his mind...or heart.

He could still see her face as she'd smiled up at him beneath the fireworks display two nights ago. It had been a surprise to see her there. He hadn't heard from her since she and Oliver had left Pine Creek Farm weeks prior, and he'd had to stop himself on many occasions from texting or calling her.

Each time he was tempted, he reminded himself that she'd asked for space and time, and that he'd agreed to give it to her. He had no idea what the time they'd spent apart had done for Mallory's feelings for him, but it had certainly cemented his feelings for her.

The house felt empty and lonely without her and Oliver. But it went far beyond that. He missed seeing her smile first thing every morning, bumping into her as they cooked breakfast and sitting peacefully by her side under the stars every evening. None of those memories had anything to do with Oliver but had everything to do with Mallory.

From the moment he'd first met her, she'd tugged at his heart. Initially, out of empathy but later, out of love.

He loved Mallory, with or without Oliver. But he'd rather it be with.

He'd wondered often over the past several weeks how Oliver was doing. Whether he'd grown, had begun developing new skills or if he still smiled often. He missed him so much and had, many times, thought of calling Mallory and accepting her offer to spend time with him. But that wouldn't do. Not when Mallory was under the impression that he only loved her because of Oliver.

It was Mallory who he wanted to see and he hoped she would realize that.

He thought she had, actually, when he'd spotted her in the field under the fireworks display on the Fourth of July. For a moment, he thought she'd returned to tell him she'd changed her mind. He thought she would tell him that she'd decided to stay. And the disappointment in her eyes when he'd had to leave had given him hope that maybe he was right. That maybe, eventually, she would decide to return to Pine Creek Farm.

But she hadn't called. She hadn't reached out at all since that night.

It wasn't a good sign in terms of her having changed her mind.

Sighing, he rubbed his forehead then led Sugar into the stable. He took his time untacking, washing and brushing her. And after settling her in her stall, he lingered there, stroking her neck and back, praising her softly, and even taking the time to pet Miss Priss when she wound around his ankles.

He'd grown to love that cat. If nothing else, she reminded him of Mallory.

After a while, the sun dipped low against the horizon and the hands had knocked off for the day. Liam reluctantly made his way back to the main house, knowing what lay ahead of him. Every night since Mallory and Oliver had left had been lonely and, most nights, sleepless.

His heart just couldn't settle.

As he walked inside, the aroma of vegetable soup filled his lungs and he followed it to the kitchen. Nancy, the housekeeper he'd hired two weeks ago, was pouring a glass of sweet tea and placing it on the table by one place setting.

"I made soup tonight," she said, smiling. "I remember you mentioned that you like vegetable beef so I used one of your mother's recipes and whipped up a batch. There's cornbread, too, and sweet tea and cobbler for dessert." She untied the apron she wore, lifted it over her head and hung it on a hook by the refrigerator. "I'll be off then. Is there anything else you need before I go?"

Liam shook his head. "No, thank you. You've taken care of everything here, as always."

Nancy nodded and headed for the front door. "I'll be going then. My grandbabies are coming home this weekend so I need to tidy up my place, too."

"I hope you have a good visit with them," Liam said.

"Oh, I will," she said as she left, closing the front door behind her.

Liam chuckled at the thought of Nancy chasing around her young grandchildren. Nancy was in her mid-sixties, made the best lemonade and hula-hooped for exercise— he'd stumbled upon her routine in the front lawn when returning from the stable last week. All things considered, she probably made her grandchildren very happy.

Liam picked up a bowl from the table, carried it to the stove and dipped several spoonfuls of soup into the bowl. He returned to the table and sat down but after two bites of soup, his appetite vanished, as usual, and he sat back in his chair and closed his eyes, the silence in the house almost deafening.

He prayed every night for guidance, for what he should do to convince Mallory that he loved her. To find a way to reconnect with her and encourage her to give him another chance.

But she wanted space and hadn't called. Short of not respecting her wishes—which he wouldn't do—he didn't know what else he could do...except try to accept that God's plan for his future might not include Mallory.

He stood abruptly, carried his bowl to the sink, and set it down. There was no need to linger. He wasn't in the mood for dinner. Instead, he walked outside and went to the back of the house to the firepit, sat down in his chair and closed his eyes. The air was soothing, filled with the chirps and croaks of crickets and toads and the sweet scent of honeysuckle. It would be a perfect summer night, that was, if Mallory were there.

"Mind if I join you?"

He stilled at the sound of her voice.

"I've been told I have a permanent invitation," she added softly.

Liam stood and turned slowly, his gaze moving over her, taking in every detail. She wore shorts, sandals and a short-sleeve shirt. Her hair was loose, falling in waves about her shoulders. There was hope in her eyes and gentleness in her voice. She never looked more beautiful.

"I knocked on the front door, but you didn't answer," she said, "so I took a chance, hoping you were out here."

"I am."

She smiled slowly. "I see that."

Cheeks heating, he laughed as he met her eyes, hope swelling within his chest. "Did you just come for a quick visit?" he asked hesitantly. "Or do you have time to stay a while? If you're hungry, my housekeeper left a big batch of soup and cornbread." He smiled. "You're welcome to come in and join me. It'd be like old times."

"Like the night we first met," she said, smiling softly. "That sounds nice, but—" she moved closer, walking gingerly down the path and edging between the two chairs to stand in front of him "—I didn't come for dinner. I came because I was hoping we could discuss the future."

He bit his lip, almost scared to speak in case he scared her off or spoiled the moment.

"I've been thinking," she said, pushing her hands into her pockets. "About how much I love it here and how much I love you."

His breath caught and he smiled. "You love me?"

"Yes," she whispered.

She moved even closer then and one of her hands left her pocket, lifting toward him, her fist unfurling. A ring, a plain wedding band, rested in the center of her palm.

"It's not much," she whispered. "But it's the best I could

afford. I'm starting over, you see? There are three things in my life that are valuable to me. One is my faith, which led me to a new life. The second is Oliver."

"And the third?" he asked.

"The third is you," she said softly. "I love you, Liam. And if you still feel the same," she said hesitantly, "I'd love to start a new life together with you."

He smiled, his heart fit to burst. "Are you asking me to marry you?"

She nodded, her hand trembling. "Yes."

He cupped her hand in his, removed the ring with his other hand and kissed the center of her palm. He glanced up at her, the excited relief in her eyes making him smile even wider. "There's nothing I want more in this world."

Epilogue

The next year, August arrived at Pine Creek Farm and with it came a new tradition.

"What does the winner get, Uncle Liam?" Cody called out from where he stood beneath the weeping willow by the pond.

Liam smiled. "A mess of fried fish," he shouted back.

Cody, seemingly pleased with this answer, turned back to his brother, picked up his fishing pole and cast his line out into the water.

It was a beautiful summer day. There wasn't a cloud in the sky, the sun shone bright and the birds were singing. Even the weeping willow tree's branches danced in the breeze as though it were celebrating. It was a perfect afternoon for the first annual Williams family reunion.

"Dada."

Liam glanced down to where Oliver, holding tightly to both of Liam's hands, stood, balancing carefully in the grass. He was over a year old now and getting around pretty well. Liam had had to childproof just about everything inside the main house. Oliver was a curious little boy and enjoyed investigating everything he could get his hands on.

"Dada!" Oliver released Liam's hands and stretched out his arms in the universal sign of wanting to be picked up.

Liam's heart melted and he bent over, lifted Oliver up and settled him on his hip. "That's my boy," he said, kissing Oliver's cheek.

Even though Oliver had been calling him *Dad* for a couple of months now, he still felt an overwhelming sense of gratitude each time he heard Oliver say it. It was like a dream being a father. One of the greatest gifts God had given him.

"Did you save me a seat?"

Liam grinned and turned around. But the sweetest—oh, the sweetest!—gift of all was Mallory.

She strolled across the field toward him and Oliver, looking more beautiful than ever. Her wavy hair was loose, shining beneath the summer sunlight, and freckles—the cutest he'd ever seen—were sprinkled across her nose and cheeks.

It was the sun that did it. Several months ago, not long after they were married, she'd asked Liam to give her riding lessons. She'd been a natural and it hadn't taken long for her to begin participating in the trail rides he led at least twice a week and the more she rode, the more freckles appeared.

He cherished those afternoons, riding horses beneath the sun with her by his side. But his favorite part of each day was still their evenings spent by the firepit, sitting peacefully under the stars, holding hands and thanking God for the many blessings that continued to multiply in their lives.

Like today. Today, he not only had his wife and child by his side, but his brother, Jessie and their children, too. The farm was full of life and laughter and Gayle would be proud of them all.

"I was hoping we could get a clear view of the first annual fishing tournament," she said now, grinning.

"I saved the best seat in the house for us," Liam said, holding out his hand.

She slipped her hand in his and he led the way across the grass to a blanket he'd spread on a low hill that sloped just above the pond.

"Any clear winner yet?" she asked, sitting on the blanket.

"Not yet," he said as he settled Oliver onto her lap. "But there's a clear leader. Holt and the boys are neck and neck—each of them brought in three bream so far." He sat down behind Mallory and stretched out his legs, scooting close and smiling as she leaned back against his chest. "But Jessie and Ava have all three of them beat at the moment though. They've snagged at least twice as many as that already."

Mallory tipped her head back and smiled up at him. "Well, there's plenty of time for the boys to pull it off. We haven't reached the end of the contest yet."

Liam kissed her softly then wrapped his arms around her and Oliver, pulling them close, holding them safe in his arms and heart. "Yeah," he whispered, thinking of the many years ahead that would be filled with love and laughter. "This is just the beginning."

* * * * *

Dear Reader,

When I was a kid, my favorite person in the world (aside from my mom) was my grandmother. We played cards, sang songs and snapped beans on the front porch. She'd let me slip on her high heels, throw one of her silk robes over my swimsuit and jump over the oscillating sprinkler in the backyard. When I stayed overnight, we'd share a bowl of ice cream before bed, and I'd fall asleep on her shag carpet in front of the TV while she watched her "stories."

At Granny's house, I could be myself and do no wrong. And when something did go wrong or my heart was broken, I knew it was okay to cry. Because I knew she'd pull me onto her lap, wrap me in an afghan she'd knitted and soothe away my tears.

Her home was always warm and welcoming, good food was always in the fridge or on the table and I always felt safe sleeping under that roof. Every visit started with a warm hug and ended with a kiss goodbye, and always—always!—I had to promise to return.

I hope you've had someone like that in your life. And if you haven't, you can still have that now. God is the greatest protector of all.

In *A Protector for Her Baby*, Mallory follows God's lead and finds strength, a home...and Liam.

As always, thank you for reading!
April

HARLEQUIN
Reader Service

Enjoyed your book?

Try the perfect subscription for Romance readers and get more great books like this delivered right to your door.

See why over 10+ million readers have tried Harlequin Reader Service.

Start with a Free Welcome Collection with free books and a gift—valued over $20.

Choose any series in print or ebook.
See website for details and order today:

TryReaderService.com/subscriptions

RSBPA24R